Double-Barrel Horror

Amanda Hard, K. Trap Jones, Vic Kerry, J.C. Michael, The Sisters of Slaughter and Matthew Weber

edited by Matthew Weber

Double-Barrel Horror *is a collection of fictional horror stories. The tales presented here are intended to disturb. They are likely to include death, graphic violence, profanity, sexual content and other themes and images that commonly disturb. If you can't deal with these themes in your fiction, then you should avoid this book.*

Contents

Pint Bottle Press
99¢
DOUBLE-BARREL
HORROR
Chef & the Maiden
These Things We Do For Our Children
AMANDA HARD

Chef and the Maiden

by Amanda Hard

"I'm pretty hardcore, Darius," the girl told him as she flipped open a butterfly knife. "I mean, I don't want to scare you, first thing. But you need to understand a few things about me."

The man driving in the seat beside her nodded his shaven head. He understood that without carrying an assault rifle, she was as hardcore as an upper-middle class white girl could be these days, and she was cute in a kind of exhausted way that made him want to buy her a coffee before getting her naked. She smelled of an expensive lavender soap that didn't quite mask the subtle, unwashed scent characteristic of street kids.

"Deep," he said, looking at the scars in her eyes rather than on her arms.

"No, you can't go too deep or you risk hitting an artery. You have to stay just on the surface of the skin. It's an art."

"That makes you an artist," he said. "I get it. I'm an artist too, but in a different way."

She drew the blade repeatedly across the top of her bicep, over and over in short strokes. "Mmmyeah? What kind of art?"

"Culinary," he said. When she didn't respond he volunteered, "Like, cooking."

"Yeah, I figured that from the ad. Is that really an art? I thought it was something you did to keep from starving."

"It's a little more complicated than it sounds," he said. Thin lines of blood welled up from the cuts in her arm and made him salivate. "I use different materials than most cooks."

"What, like weird vegetables and tofu and stuff?" She continued to cut, largely ignoring him.

"Not quite. Different proteins. I like to experiment."

"You mean like pork?" she asked, still more focused on the cutting than she was on him. "The other white meat?"

"Like that, yes."

She grinned and the smile reached all the way to her eyes this time. That was what entranced him, that smile.

"Seen enough?" she asked. He nodded.

"Why do you do it? Cut yourself, I mean."

She flipped the knife closed and dropped it to the floorboard of the car. With a shrug, she angled her body toward his and rubbed her cheek back and forth against the vinyl of the seat. She stared at the dashboard and said simply, "Control."

He nodded slowly. She brought her gaze up to his eyes. "It's the only pain I can control," she said. "I giveth and I taketh away. It's all up to me."

He shook his head. "You're so young," he said. "Too young to know that kind of pain."

"Yeah well, you don't know the half of it," she said with a sigh.

He waited for her to launch into an over-dramatized condemnation of her so-called life. Or to hear how mean her parents, teachers or school friends were. She didn't elaborate.

He waited for a few soundless moments before venturing a guess. "So was it your dad or your stepdad?"

It was almost always one or the other with these girls. He looked at Sarah, still bleeding ever so slightly in the seat next to him, and thought she might actually be different. She was unsullied in the most basic ways: clean record, clean veins, clean fingernails. He hardened a little as he pictured her in a gauze dress and no underwear, her small breasts unfettered under the cloth, the black and white skin of their intertwined legs a brilliant chiaroscuro of flesh.

"Mom's boyfriend. Shows what you know." She smirked at him but kept his gaze. "He wasn't bad looking, and if he hadn't been doing my mother, I might have hooked up with him when I was old enough." She shrugged again then dropped her eyes. "There's something a little gross about sharing a guy with the woman who gave birth to you."

He waited for her to look up at him and judge his reaction to this news. When she didn't, he knew she was telling the truth.

"I can appreciate that," he said, careful to not imply understanding. That turned the truthful ones away almost immediately. At the next stop light he retrieved her knife from the floor and opened it. He flipped it around briefly, unsuccessfully trying to match her earlier display of dexterity, before offering it back to her as the light changed.

She donned an exasperated look, took the knife, and demonstrated the trick. The blade was a flashing speck of silver as she whipped it around and around its handles, the afternoon sun glinting on the supremely sharpened metal. This was a knife that could effortlessly slice through paper, would accept no resistance from bone, and promised to neatly separate two ends of a joint. She raised her eyes to his.

"You gotta be careful with it, keep it clean. I don't wanna get Hep-C."

"How do you keep it so sharp?" he asked.

"I sharpen it, dipshit." Her eyes laughed at him. She started to smile then seemed to think better of it. "So, what's with the ad? You ever gonna tell me?"

This girl, the black-haired, blue-eyed Goth "Sarah," or so she claimed, meant the Craigslist ad he had placed online a week before. Sarah's predecessors had responded to voicemail-based dating ads, personal ads in newspapers and singles magazines, even flyers tacked to adult bookstore bulletin boards. Those were the dangerous days, he remembered. Everything was so much easier now and even more anonymous, with the internet. Now you just had to watch out for cell phones and the narrow sweep of security cameras. Make sure nobody was filming you. Make sure you didn't end up on YouTube and then in jail.

"Yes, but first we get ice cream." He turned the key and revved the Camaro's engine. She rolled her eyes but smiled at him. It was worth the risk, that smile.

"I'm not a child," she said, trying to look offended.

"Ice cream used to be a delicacy. It was very difficult to make, and expensive. You wouldn't waste it on children."

"Aren't you supposed to save dessert for after dinner?" Her seatbelt was unbuckled, and she opened her legs a little wider, taking up a little more space on the seat and bringing her thigh closer to his. The crotch of his jeans tightened uncomfortably, and he dropped his right hand down to her knee, which poked out of a gash in her jeans like a white bone from torn skin. Her fingertips found his and brushed over his knuckles. He shuddered from the sensation and the anticipation of feeling more of her skin against his. He didn't answer her; he was afraid his voice would break or that he would say something stupid. That lavender scent rolled off her in waves, as she moved. The cloying odor, combined with her touch, was intoxicating.

"I know cooking is an art," she said. "I didn't mean to be rude." She squeezed his hand, but his throat was tight and he couldn't respond. He kept his eyes on the road and nodded, a gesture he hoped she would interpret as disinterested and cool. He allowed his hand to rest more heavily on her leg, and as they drove in silence he drew it slowly up around the curve of her inner thigh. His fingers reached out, almost touching the seam of her pants, slowly creeping closer to that sweet triangle he imagined, but she gasped and pulled his hand away. Panting softly, she closed her legs to him, but returned her fingers to his, intertwining them and squeezing as if in apology. He glanced over at the curtain of badly-dyed black hair hiding her face and decided to forego the ice cream.

"So what's the special menu, D?" she finally asked.

"What?" He momentarily forgot the text of the ad that had brought her to him.

"You wanted a hookup with somebody who would appreciate a special menu. What is it? Is it a sex thing? I don't know the reference, so you'll have to educate me." She squeezed his hand again, lightly dragging her fingers over his palm. He shivered.

"Sarah, you aren't a prostitute, are you?"

She surprised him, again. "There's a first for everything, I guess. But as of..." she looked down at her watch, "uh, three this afternoon, I am not. Of course, that answer really depends on you." She raised her eyebrows expectantly and waited for him to deny it.

"How do you mean?"

"Well, are you looking for a girlfriend or for a one-night date?"

"I enjoy cooking and I enjoy obscure recipes and techniques, so I'm just looking for someone to share that with."

"I don't really want a steady boyfriend, you know." Her smile faded, and the sunlight angling in from the windshield made her eyes narrow. She looked too young, and too sad. He realized he was going to have to get her out to the house quickly before he lost his nerve.

"Let's not put the cart before the horse, okay? It's one date, not a marriage proposal." He steadied the wheel with his knee and nudged her playfully on the shoulder with his hand. She didn't move. She was solid against his touch, an immovable object in the passenger seat. He tried to smile, but his resolve was failing. What if she was too strong? What if she had a phone with a GPS tracker?

"Everything is back at the house. It won't take long to prepare," he told her, presenting a sense of purpose he didn't really feel. "We'll be there shortly. I'll open up a bottle of wine and you can relax."

"I'm pretty relaxed here." She closed her eyes to illustrate the point. She kept her lips slightly apart, a trusting nymphette who wasn't paying attention to where they were going or what turns they took. He smiled and told himself it would be easy. The erection which had earlier threatened to betray his interest returned, stronger and angrier. The swelling in his crotch was almost painful, and when he shifted in his seat to relieve the pressure, Sarah opened her eyes and withdrew her hand from his, using it to scratch at the uneven layers of hair hanging down the back of her neck.

"I'm not eating rocky mountain oysters or pig balls or whatever you call them, just so you know. If that's on the menu then you can turn around right now and take me back."

"No balls," he said, his erection gaining enthusiasm. "I promise." He turned the Camaro down a dirt road almost hidden by trees and vines, then followed the narrow path to a well-hidden farmhouse waiting patiently behind the tree line. "We're here now, so why don't you go in and make yourself comfortable. The front door's unlocked. I gotta get some things out of the back of the car."

She swung her legs over the seat and opened the door before he'd even pulled the emergency brake. Leveraging herself up and out of the seat by holding onto the top of the door frame, she moved like an old woman. Slow, grim and determined. The grass was high, and he watched her shuffle her flat sneakers through it as she made her way to the door.

When she was safely inside, he opened the trunk and pulled out his "kit." Among other things, the canvas bag held chloroform, a ball gag, paper plates and napkins, and mismatched plastic cutlery. It was always a shame, eating off those cheap plastic dishes, when he could be dining on a place setting of the fine china left to him by his grandmother. But paper burned quickly and left no easily recovered DNA behind, and truth be told he hated washing dishes anyway. He upended the bottle of chloroform on a rag, stoppered it, threw it back in the bag, and slammed the trunk lid.

He found her in the kitchen, going through the cabinets.

"This has got to be the plainest set of dishes I've ever seen," she called over her shoulder. "No flowers, no curly-Qs, no color. Looks like what they'd use at an Olive Garden or something." She leaned back against him as he came up behind her, and didn't even try to kick him when he brought the rag up to her face and held it, waiting. The chloroform's acrid scent was hidden by the sudden cloud of lavender drifting up from her limp body. He inhaled as deeply as he could without making himself nauseous, then dragged her over to the prep station he'd previously set up by the long wooden dining table.

Between the pounding of his heart, the throbbing of his cock, and the gurgling and growling of his stomach, he could barely focus on the task at hand. He lit the oven and pulled a cast-iron skillet down from the hanging rack. Seasoning it with a little butter, he set it on a low flame, then unrolled a canvas knife bag on the table and tried to remember how long it usually took to sauté asparagus.

***

Sarah really was different. He decided this when she didn't cry, scream or beg for her life—unlike the other dozen women who had enjoyed his catering and gourmet dinners. When she came to, she simply looked around, took in the details of the kitchen: the long dining table decorated with a yellow tablecloth, the blue and yellow sunflower placemat, the brilliant white tile floor, and the wooden chair her hands were tied to. Her eyes didn't even widen when Darius showed her the butterfly knife and clumsily opened it in front of her.

"Be careful with it," was all she said. "You gotta keep it clean."

"I'm going to use this to cut off your clothes," he explained. "So don't squirm or thrash around. I don't want to—" he started to say "cut you" but that was the complete opposite of the truth. He wanted very badly to slice into that perfect pinkish flesh. He desperately wanted to see the tiny trails of blood she had elicited earlier. He needed to see them. To lick them clean. To taste the broken skin underneath.

She nodded, then sat perfectly still as he drew the blade across the seams of her shirt and slit the straps of her bra. The white of her chest spilled out from the ruins of the black tshirt the way the sun emerged from the dark clouds of a summer storm. But even as he gasped at the beauty of those delicate breasts, he was appalled by the flesh surrounding them.

Ringing her upper arms and circling under the swell of her nipples were dozens of dark red scars, relics of insults long past, pain gone but not forgotten—concentric arcs of her own angry memories, carved in her own flesh by her own steady hand. She was like a tattooed Maori warrior, and as he stared, the spirals seemed to hypnotize him.

"There are more," she said quietly. "If you want to see them. Different ones."

He nodded in silence, still awed by the illustrations of her troubled short life. He slipped the knife under the cuff of her jeans and drew it upward, watching more pink and red circles appear as the material covering them fell away. The closer he got to her crotch, the deeper and redder the scars. She gasped, although whether in pain or fear he wasn't sure, as the fabric separated and revealed open gashes across her inner thighs where the skin had been not only split but removed in thin slices. Ribbons of raw flesh alternated with neat but gaping gaps an eighth-inch thick in her skin—gaps which oozed trickles of black blood and a pink pus as the tissue tried to heal itself from the inside. The edges of the larger gashes were black from an amateur attempt at cauterization. He was horrified by the beauty of it; entranced by the hideous roiling movement of the rings as she flexed and relaxed her thighs.

"The other leg, is it...?" he began. Her face was serene, and when she flashed that dazzling smile at him, he felt himself falling. He landed on his knees in front of her, dizzy and slightly sick to his stomach. Her jeans had been washed in the scent of lavender. Without that disguise, a stench wafted up from the open wounds: a sour smell of rot and pus. Part of him wanted to gag; another part wanted to lick the wounds clean as he washed and scrubbed her tortured skin with his tongue, alternating between the cuts and her clitoris while she moaned underneath him.

"Not as much," she answered. "There's still plenty left to do." She uncrossed her feet, and stretched out her naked leg towards him. She circled her ankle and the sneaker fell off, leaving behind a white foot dotted and ringed with trial cuts, obviously some of the first she'd made, and not as neatly organized as those on her limbs and torso.

"I only learned about flaying a little while ago," she explained. "It's tricky. Real easy to get an infection." She rested her scarred foot on his thigh and he tried very hard not to recoil. "I always just flushed the pieces. I never really thought about what I was doing until I saw your ad."

He used the side of his hand to push her foot away. With the other hand he slit the rest of her jeans away, one long cut across her low belly severing the two halves, and let the pieces fall to the floor. She wore simple pink cotton briefs that, when he cut them off, revealed a bald crotch covered in dark red and black spirals of flesh and no flesh. Without the lavenderdrenched fabric to counter it, the stench of the wounds was overpowering. He rocked backward, trying to breathe cleaner air and settle his stomach.

"The ad … that was pretty see-through, you know," she said. "And when I saw you, I knew you had to be up to something. You're hot. And built. Not the kind of guy who you'd imagine advertising for a hookup, unless..." she trailed off and slowly smiled at him. The central features of that smile were less innocent, and the juncture of smile and eyes crinkled in a much older and more jaded way now.

"Unless what?" he asked, the knife in his hand, and a heavy feeling in his belly that wasn't quite hunger.

"Unless your personal tastes were a little too ... exotic for the average girl? Maybe a little dangerous?"

A wave of heat passed over Darius, and he realized the oven had been at temperature for some time. He needed to get the main entree cooking soon, or it would throw off the finish time for the side dishes.

"I guess I'm not exactly average though, am I?" she asked.

He shook his head. Looking in her eyes made him uncomfortable, but he couldn't stand looking at those scars another minute. He felt his ardor deflating, replaced by a sense of repulsion. Frankly, every word she spoke made him want to be somewhere else, farther and farther away from her and her hideous self-cut tattoos.

"I told you I was hardcore," she said.

"Yeah, you did." He wiped his forehead with the back of his hand.

She stretched, arching her back gently and speaking slowly. "So have you ever actually had a date where you *both* enjoyed the main course?"

He shook his head and frowned. He should have put the ball gag on her.

"Would you like to?" she said softly.

He couldn't help the smile that crossed his lips. It was partly a grimace, a reaction to the gruesome scene playing out at his table. But there was, he had to admit, a certain amount of genuine joy in it. She would have been beautiful without her disfigurement, her muscles long and lean, uncut skin fresh and clear. Watching her eat her own perfect flesh could be heavenly. That she was threatening to enjoy it was the pinnacle of every fantasy he'd ever dreamed in his kitchen.

He allowed the smile to grow wider as he felt himself stiffening again.

She wiggled her shoulders and fingers, looking back at him, her eyebrows raised. She rubbed the side of her cheek against the wood post of the chair back, scratching gently. "Let me do it," she said softly. "I can make it last."

Closing his eyes against the heat in the room, her words echoed in his imagination. "I can make it last," she said, again and again, and her foul smell blended with the aroma of sizzling butter to create a salty-sweet heaviness in the warm air. He salivated visibly, drips of it spilling over his bottom lip to fall onto his shirt. He wiped his mouth and opened his eyes. Sawing with the kind of frenzied motion he usually saved for pumping his dick after a fine dinner, he ripped the knife across the nylon ropes binding her to the chair. When the pieces of rope fell to the ground, she rubbed her wrists and smiled at him again. Then she took charge, the new kitchen manager setting the itinerary for the evening.

"You'll want to wash that off," she said, quickly adding, "You're probably the same way about your own knives, right?"

Darius nodded and took the knife to the sink, where he sprayed it down with hot water. When he turned back to her, she was standing by his prep station, looking curiously at the raw vegetables still in their bags.

"You want me to help cut these up?" She asked as if it was the most normal thing in the world—as if she was asking if he wanted fries with that, or if he knew the time. He shook his head and handed her the wet knife. She took it and went back to the table, where she sat down on the placemat, spread her naked legs and examined the lesser scarred thigh. She looked up at him. "Do you want to watch?"

He did. He absolutely did not. He didn't know what he wanted. This night was not going as planned. He was afraid of what he might say, so he just responded, "I have to prep the vegetables."

"Can I have a plate to put it on?" she asked, innocently, as if asking for a tissue. He went to the cabinet, lifted out an oblong china serving dish and presented it to her. She had already begun preliminary edging on what would be the first large cut, and blood seeped out onto the placemat. He wanted to pull her down off what had been a fastidiously clean table only a few hours before. Wanted to slit her throat and leave her for the carrion animals to dispose of. Wanted to be rid of her and her lavender stink and her spirals and arcs of blood and scars, but those spirals were cobra's eyes, entrancing and hypnotizing. He wanted to get back his normal thoughts, focus on cooking this fine dinner he'd planned for months, and be rid of her temptations. But as much as he tried to look away, he found he couldn't.

"That's a batonnet cut," he heard himself telling her, from a memory a million years ago, when he'd learned to cook Beef Bourguignon—a time when he could still eat beef and be satisfied. A time before whatever had happened to his brain that resulted in these cravings. Or maybe he'd been born this way? He couldn't remember.

"I can do a Julienne, like French fries." She exhaled through her nose, so that the last words came out as a snort. She slid the knife deeper, into another layer of skin, and gasped softly as she drew the blade toward her. "The pain is amazing, only…" She stopped, removing the blade and swallowing. "It doesn't go away quickly. Can I have a glass of water?" Her face paled and her lips trembled. He poured water for her from a glass pitcher in the refrigerator and before he realized his mistake, let her drink from an actual crystal glass. Prints, DNA. What was he thinking? Now he'd have to destroy it, and that was a set he liked.

She swallowed all the water and handed the glass back to him. Then she set to work on the edges of the wound, releasing a thin rectangle of flesh from the rest. Moaning loudly, she loosened the edges from the layers of skin underneath, and with a minute flick and an even louder moan, held out a thin pink and red worm on the edge of the knife—beads of sweat on her white brow, and a triumphant smile on her face.

"First bite," she said weakly and flipped the slice of her own skin onto the plate. He wanted to fry it in butter immediately—damn the sides and the vegetables! But he waited patiently as she stripped away another piece of skin. He brought her a wet towel to wipe away the blood, and waited as she made more cuts, contributed more slices to the plate. The kitchen was full of the smell of blood and butter. A hot fury burned in the gas oven, while the skillet baked on the range top.

"You should let me do you," she whispered between incisions. "Then you could cook the two pieces together and we could share it."

Sweat poured down the skin of his neck, whether from the heat or her suggestion he wasn't sure. What would it feel like, eating his own flesh? Cutting into his own skin and frying it in butter? Each piece exquisitely batonnet cut, salted and floured, and finally sautéed to a perfect medium? But he couldn't trust her to cut him. She wasn't trained; he would do it himself.

"Show me," he said.

She smiled. "Take off your jeans." Her face was pale, but her eyes were radiant.

He stripped out of his jeans and dropped them on the floor. Sitting in the chair she had been tied to, he faced her: legs spread, his erection poking up from his briefs. His dark thighs trembled as her hands brushed along them, feeling the soft hairless skin at the crease of the underwear. She bent over his lap, breathing her warm breath on his crotch.

"I have to find the right spot," she murmured. He pressed his groin upward to meet her lips, and she laughed. "Here, along the edge here. At the hairline. You can cut here." She pointed to a spot paralleling the seam of his briefs. Her fingers were close enough he could feel their warmth. He nodded and took the knife she offered him. She'd locked the handles so he wouldn't accidentally slip and cut off his own dick. She was thoughtful; he liked that about her.

"Lightly at first," she explained. "Trace the line. Then go back and make it heavier." She put her hand over his and squeezed gently. "It won't hurt at first. Use that moment to gain momentum, you know what I mean?" He did and nodded. She smiled again. "Go ahead. The first one's the hardest."

He took a deep breath and wiped sweat from his forehead with the back of his hand. He remembered the months of cooking school where he'd practiced butchery on sides of pig, lamb, cow. Never human. He was about to go where no member of his graduating class had ever gone. Where none of the smartass chef teachers ever thought to go. He exhaled slowly and went—slicing deep into his own dark brown skin, while his own bright red blood bubbled out from the rupture in his flesh.

The pain was exquisite. Intense. Almost unbearable. He grimaced silently, and she squeezed his other knee.

"You can do it. Push yourself."

He pushed. He pushed the knife into his groin, parallel to the first cut, as she'd directed. The pain didn't change. It was excruciating, but it was his pain and he knew he could take it away at any time. She took a towel and wiped his leg. Under the blood, two perfect cuts were clearly visible for a brief moment before the blood occluded them again. She smiled at him, nodding her praise, wiping away blood again and again. He cut again, two more times, deepening the first two.

"Square it off now, do the edges," she said. "And then lift it out with the knife."

She didn't smell so bad anymore. He remembered her smelling of lavender. He tried to take a deep breath, but it was so much work. He wasn't smelling lavender, he realized. It was the same coppery tang from before; blood, with a touch of smoke—the singular flavor of burned food. He looked back at the stove and remembered with a pang of regret that he'd left butter in the skillet. The stove was so far away, the butter already burned. No point in trying to do anything about it now. He closed his eyes. He still had two more cuts to make. The knife fell from his hand and clattered to the floor. Beneath heavy lids, he saw the girl jump down from the table to retrieve it. A moment later he felt another cut, almost painless this time, in his other thigh. A long slice, slow and patient. She would have made a good chef, he thought, trying to remember the taste of his favorite wine, the one he usually paired with women. His last thought, before blacking out, was to wonder if this girl would have tasted different from the other. He decided she would have, and some part of him mourned her untasted flesh before he finally collapsed on the floor in a lake of his own dark blood.

Sarah walked slowly over to the stove, the platter in her hand heaped with small slivers of pink meat that quivered in their gelatinous red marinade as she stepped. She placed the platter down on the counter and dropped another dollop of butter into the black skillet, which sizzled and melted almost immediately. She turned down the fire and searched through the canisters for the one containing flour. She dumped several cups of flour onto the platter and dragged the slices of meat around in spiral trails until they were covered completely in white. A little salt, a little pepper, a little garlic powder in the mix, and she dropped the dusty white strips into the skillet.

She burned the first batch and threw them aside. She cooked the second batch until the springy quality of the meat matched that of chicken. This too was overdone, and she tossed them aside with the others. The third batch, however, was perfect. The sweet crispy fat crunched against her teeth, but melted quickly in her mouth and dribbled down the back of her throat, leaving a rich coating on her tongue that reminded her of how freshly steamed beef heart left its greasy trail in her mouth.

"Interesting experiment, Darius," she told his cooling body, "but not worth the effort, really." She took another bite and threw the rest of the uncooked skin in the skillet. She turned the flame up to maximum and watched as the heat evaporated the fat and flames licked the edges of the pan. She dropped the towels she'd used near the pan and smiled as the fire found a new fuel, burning a path across the counter and up to the wooden cabinets above. In moments the entire kitchen was ablaze.

"I warned you not to go too deep." She gathered her shredded clothes and wrapped the tablecloth around her naked body. She grabbed the keys to the car from the counter where Darius had left them, then turned and padded slowly away from the inferno consuming the farmhouse. She climbed into the Camaro and adjusted the rearview mirror for her height. She gave the smoke and flames of the farmhouse one last look before speeding out onto the highway.

"I told you I was hardcore," she whispered.

These Things We Do for Our Children

by Amanda Hard

From the outside, Miami's oldest botanica wasn't noticeably different from any other. Tall racks full of saints' candles formed pillars in the front of the store. Long squat shelves housed plaster statues of thin, frail Christs and porcelain Virgin Marys. Both side walls were devoted to packages of oils and powders, homemade soaps and bath salts, incense and perfumes. The only real difference was the back room, hidden from customers by a heavy blue curtain behind which the muffled chittering of an excited conversation could usually be heard.

The pale-haired and middle-aged white woman browsing the incense display was a shop regular. She smiled at the young man emerging from the darkness behind the curtain, his dark eyes glittering with mischief.

"Miss Elizabeth, you look as beautiful as the golden sun," he said, opening his arms in welcome. "Please forgive my manners. I did not realize we had a date tonight." Elizabeth giggled.

Maria, the store owner, hissed at him from behind the register.

Allesandro was a tall, good-looking boy in his twenties and undoubtedly a heartbreaker in the community. He acted as bodyguard and personal assistant for his mother, Carmen, who read palms and tarot cards in the back room of the store on Tuesday nights. She'd read Elizabeth's fortune on several occasions, and each time Elizabeth had moved the conversation one step closer to the subject of her long and exhausting search—a search which confirmed her belief that the *Botanica San Gertrude* was the resting place of the item she so desperately needed. Allesandro's presence seemed to confirm it.

"Oh you," she playfully swatted his arm. "I'm here to see your mother."

Pretending heartbreak, Allesandro led her back behind the curtain. A round and jolly woman with uneven bangs and fake eyelashes acknowledged Elizabeth with a smile and shooed the boy away.

"It's my Miss Lizabeth. Is good to see you again. I read the cards for you, okay?"

Elizabeth took her usual seat across the table. "Actually, I didn't come for a reading tonight."

"I do it anyway," Carmen said, gathering the cards with a graceful swoop of her hand. She hummed under her breath as she shuffled them, then dropped the first ten cards into their positions with minute flicks of her wrist. She bent over them, studying the picture the cards formed on the table.

"Carmen, I need you to look at my face for a minute," Elizabeth said.

Carmen's eyes flickered up, but quickly dropped back down to the cards. "I don't read faces. Just hands and cards." She turned over one of the battered tarot trumps and frowned. "The Devil," she said loudly. "This is big problem for you—you chained to the past. Something you trying to drag back into the present." She tapped the Devil card with the long nail of her index finger. "We talk about this before. What I tell you then?"

"I—I don't really want a reading, Carmen. I'm looking for something else tonight, please."

"There's a boy," Carmen said, looking confused. She stared up at Elizabeth's lined and tired face. "*Chica*, you got a young boyfriend you not tell me about, or you just got hot pants for 'Sandro?" She laughed out loud, slapping the table with the palm of her hand. Elizabeth jumped at the sound.

"Carmen, I really wanted to purchase something tonight," Elizabeth tried again.

"Go tell Maria and she get it for you."

"No, I want to buy it from you. Maria won't sell it to me. But you—you'll understand. You know I won't do anything bad with it."

Carmen frowned and sat back in her chair. She crossed her arms over her bosom and looked directly into Elizabeth's eyes. She took a long, deep inhale of breath, and then blew it out through pursed lips.

"No," she said flatly. "I won't do it." She emphasized this decision with a firm shake of her head. "I won't sell you a love potion for my 'Sandro." She tried kept her lips together, but the laughter burst out of her nose and the edges of her mouth. She slapped the table again, guffawing loudly.

"Carmen, no." Elizabeth steeled herself, leaned in toward the table and said softly, "I need the *pata*."

Carmen's laughter died in the air. Her smile faded and she seemed to shrink, sinking deeper into her chair. Her black-rimmed eyes reflected Elizabeth's own for a moment, before hardening and dropping back down to the cards.

"No."

"Please," Elizabeth said. "You know me, you know my heart. You know I won't—"

"No," she said again. "You have good heart. Clean soul. Jesus loves you and forgive your sins. You don't want this thing. There no forgiving what you do with it."

"Carmen, I promise. No evil. Only good. I've got it all worked out. I've thought it all through. Please. I know it's here. Sell it to me."

Carmen continued to ignore her, staring at the cards.

"Please. You know I won't abuse it. I have it all worked out." She hadn't let herself consider the possibility that the sisters wouldn't sell it to her. *Please…*"

"Five thousand dollars," Carmen finally whispered. It was what Elizabeth had expected her to say, and was also the amount she had stashed in an envelope in her purse. One hundred crisp fifty dollar bills fresh from the bank that morning. The last of Elizabeth's savings. Her only hope for the future.

"I have it," she whispered.

"And you leave now. And you don't come back here. You never come back here, you got that, *Bruja*?" Carmen's eyes were narrow slits. Her mouth was a thin red gash across her unsmiling face.

"I understand." Elizabeth reached into her purse for the envelope. Carmen got up from the table and left without a word. Elizabeth waited. After a few moments, Alessandro appeared at the curtained door, holding a small package wrapped in brown paper. He motioned to Elizabeth and disappeared behind the curtain. She left the envelope on the table and followed him out to the front room of the store. The lights were off, and Maria and Carmen were gone. Without his usual grin, Alessandro handed her the bundle and opened the front door for her. She clutched it to her chest like an infant, breathing in the queer musty smell emanating from the paper wrapping.

"She doesn't want to see you again," he told her as she stepped over the threshold. "You aren't welcome here now." Elizabeth turned to face him and nodded. His face softened as he ran a hand through his hair. "I know my mother," he said, "and she won't fix it. Your mistake, I mean. You're going to come back and ask her to fix it, and she's not going to do it."

Elizabeth shook her head, determined. "I have it all worked out."

"No you don't," he said.

"I know what I'm doing."

"No. You don't."

He looked back at the shop for a moment before stepping out into the street and closing the door behind him. "Look, you know what this is, so you have to know you're not the first person to ask for one." He nodded at the package in her arms. "But you don't have to go through with it. Take it home and throw it in the fire. Save your soul."

"You aren't a mother," she said. "You can't possibly understand. Until you're a parent…" Her voice caught in her throat and she couldn't continue.

Alessandro sighed and turned his back to her. "If you do this," he said over his shoulder, "there's no going back. There's no forgiveness. No redemption when you die. You think anything is really worth that?" He closed the door on her, his question hanging in the evening air like smoke from a ring of incense.

"One thing is," she said to the door.

***

Just over three years after the notification officers appeared on her porch, Elizabeth turned her back on the closed and locked door of the botanica. She thought she could feel Alessandro's eyes on her as she walked across the street to her car, but as she drove away, the window to the shop was dark.

They always notify in person, someone once told her. They don't really send a telegram. It's always a visit. A chaplain will wait in the car, close enough to be convenient, but out of immediate eyesight, unobtrusive. He will refer to the family's religion as their "faith" and offer assistance in maintaining that faith in the wake of such a tragedy.

Elizabeth clutched the paper-wrapped package to her chest, steering with her left hand. She dropped her face down and inhaled the musty scent. *Forgive me Father, but I know what I do*, she thought. She had it all worked out, down to the details. She was going to do it right.

This was her faith.

Wish the First:

Unable to call an attorney for expert advice, Elizabeth did what she could. For the better part of a year, while conducting her search for the *pata*, she read contracts. She studied terms and conditions pages, end-user agreements, and the fine print on warranties, bills of sale, and leases. She poured over real estate contracts and loan applications, looking for loopholes and vagaries that might invalidate what she intended to do, or cause it to go horribly wrong. She knew she would have only three requests, and each had to be perfectly worded and meticulously detailed. Her success depended upon those details.

The first request would have to be money. Elizabeth had done the math. She knew how expensive counterfeit identification would be. She knew how many palms she needed to grease to arrange for safe passage, and she knew how expensive buying American citizenship would be, but it was the option that made the most sense, given the situation. Alex had always been dark-skinned. She could pass him off as a Mexican student hoping for naturalization, and eventually petition for a brand new social security number. A clean one. One without a paper trail that led back to Iraq, back to the Army, and back to the uniformed men on her porch and the flag his friends had folded into a neat triangle and presented to her in the mist.

Powerball was the obvious choice: legal, and with the taxes paid, nobody would be hurt by it. At the gas station on her way home, she filled in the tiny ovals with a borrowed pen. The numbers were anything but random: Alex's age and birthday, her age and birthday plus one, since it was a day she shared with her son. She blinked back tears as she reread the numbers, confirming them.

Elizabeth handed the clerk a dollar bill, then stuffed the freshly printed lottery ticket down into the left cup of her bra under the breast a nursing baby Alex had always preferred. She sniffed at her shirt. She could almost smell that milk again, a soft and lightly sour odor mixed with the odd musty smell from the package now tucked under the passenger seat. She left the receipt on the counter and went back to her car where she sat silently, wanting to remember the warm prickling she'd always felt when her breasts swelled with milk, but feeling only a heavy emptiness.

The realtor's sign reflected her headlights as she pulled in to her driveway. She cut the engine and went over the list of ingredients in her mind: sea salt, candles, the oils and incenses, a crucifix, a plastic water bottle of communion wine, the prayer, the knife, a small copper bowl, and the item in the package. Was she forgetting anything? She grabbed her purse and gently picked up the package, fumbling with her keys as she got out. Inside the house was dark. She walked through the hall into the kitchen and flipped on the overhead light.

A spotless floor greeted her. Empty white countertops glistened. A single appliance, a coffee maker, sat in the corner under the window, joined by a solitary white coffee mug. Everything from the cupboards had already been packed and loaded into the U-Haul, along with the contents of all the rest of the rooms—except for one. She'd saved it for last.

On the kitchen table was a rectangular box, its lid slightly askew.

She brought the package over to the table, and slowly unfolded the paper wrapping. The musty smell grew stronger as layer after layer of butcher paper fell away until she was left holding a stained linen cloth with a tiny brown object folded inside. It was a paw—a tiny and furry paw, its fingers curled in a relaxed fist, the severed stump sewn shut at the wrist. She gently lay the tiny hand down on its linen wrapping and proceeded to unpack the items from the rectangular box.

At no time did she consider the insanity of her actions. She did not think of the potentially wasted five thousand dollars, or the hundreds of hours she'd spent pouring over contracts and old manuscripts and grimoires. She didn't think of the blasphemy behind the Blood of Christ collected from seven different Masses over the last three days and surreptitiously spit into a plastic water bottle. She worked silently and emotionlessly, setting up the altar exactly the way the old books instructed. Every dimension perfectly measured, down to the millimeter. Every item exactly as described, down to the last detail. No substitutions. No mistakes.

The odor emanating from the paw seemed to grow stronger as she worked. Elizabeth poured a packet of incense over a piece of charcoal and lit it, inhaling to allow the pungent smoke to fill her nostrils and lungs. With a short stub of match, she lit a white candle then dropped the spent match into the sink. She returned to her chair and poured a small amount of one of Maria's pre-mixed oils into the palm of her hand. Silently she rubbed the fragrant oil over the remaining candles, anointing them.

The objects arranged, she began the ritual she'd handcopied and memorized months ago, performing each gesture meticulously, adding exactly the right amounts of each ingredient to the copper bowl. She spoke the words clearly and loudly, intoning and enunciating each syllable. There was no room for error.

When she sliced the knife across the palm of her hand, her voice did not waver. She allowed seven drops of her blood to fall into the water bottle, mixing with the communion wine turned Blood of Christ. She carefully dripped the bloody mixture on the small hand, filling the center of the palm as she spoke the final prayer.

"Eternal Father, I offer You the most precious blood of thy Divine Son, Jesus, in union with the Masses said throughout the world today, for all the Holy Souls in Purgatory, for sinners everywhere, for sinners in the universal church, for those in my own home and in my family. Amen."

Blood and wine soaked into the desiccated paw, and it seemed to grow larger as she watched. A candle sputtered. A second candle flared, and the incense hissed on the button of charcoal, filling the air with a cloud of violet scent.

Elizabeth made her wish.

***

Alex's room was just as he'd left it six years before. She'd been careful over those years to dust around everything so as not to disturb the fragile order in which he'd left his life behind. His closet was mostly full of boxes: childish things neatly put away when he'd enlisted in the Army. An abandoned letter sweater and three jackets were pushed to one side, squashed together to make room for a stack of plastic bins containing the detritus of his high school years. Only one box had Elizabeth ever dared open, a shoebox containing pictures of June, his high school sweetheart, and her letters—which Elizabeth could never bring herself to read. After June's disappearance, it had seemed too much of an insult to both their memories to read her intimate thoughts.

She shivered when she removed the neatly pressed quilt from the top of the bed. She'd bought it for Alex on his first day of school, and it had been his bed ever since. Some of the fabric blocks were starting to show wear, their bright colors faded and the seams between the pieces starting to unravel. She folded the quilt into a neat square and placed it at the bottom of a cardboard box. The room grew blurry as the tears she had been shedding for years formed again in her eyes and spilled out onto the bare sheets. She pressed her lips together and tried to blink the water from her eyes, but then she was crying, sobbing loudly, her mouth stretched open in a howl of anguish as her hands wiped across her face and fingers clutched her thin blonde hair. She screamed until she had no voice left. She screamed until her pain became anger once again. She didn't stop screaming until her anger focused and she found a numb calm in her chest.

The room became a task like any other. The room she had avoided for so many years, afraid to move even a single item for fear of changing the memory of the one who had lived here, was about to be packed. Elizabeth closed her mouth and dried her eyes with the sleeve of her shirt. She had work to do.

By morning, the room was as empty as the others in the house, and the U-Haul was full. Elizabeth carefully packed up the altar and wrapped each item in newspaper before stowing them all together in a storage bin. The paw she gently placed in a plastic bowl, noticing with concern that some of the hair had fallen out the night before. It gave off a rather unpleasant odor, musty but with a tinge of mildew and rot. She sealed the container and wrapped it in a towel before setting it atop the other ritual items and placing the box in the passenger seat of the U-Haul.

After taking one last look through the empty house, she found herself hesitating by the door to the kitchen. There on the wall were a series of pencil marks a few centimeters apart—a height chart showing the progression from threefoot toddler to six-foot-soldier. Her vision swam but she bit the inside of her lip to maintain control. She closed and locked the front door, turning her back on the empty house. She would make arrangements to get her car later. Right now her only focus was to get herself and that package in the front seat up to Panama City Beach.

Wish the Second:

It took weeks for the media fanfare to wind down and for Elizabeth to feel safe leaving her parking lot without a disguise. The attorney she'd hired had not agreed with her decision to take a smaller amount of the lottery money in one lump sum, but he'd stopped arguing with her when she insisted she wanted to do something charitable with the money, such as sponsoring young immigrants and helping them get their citizenship.

Elizabeth found a nice condo on the beach, a place with a greater than average number of Hispanic and mixed-race owners. She didn't look out of place, the way she'd always felt in Miami. She dyed her hair a walnut brown that flattered her pale skin, bought some new clothes, and traded in her car for a larger luxury model.

She made one last trip south to finish her business in Miami. When she headed back home and looked in her new rear-view mirror she saw the same tired eyes she'd seen every day for the last six years, but now those eyes were different.

They were hopeful. Her smile almost reached the corners of her eyes.

The sky darkened quickly as she drove, and at some point she realized a bright star hung visible in the top edge of her windshield. She wasn't good enough with astronomy to know if it was an actual star or just the planet Venus, but it made her remember Alex as a young boy, tearing out of the house after dinner to set eyes on the "wishing star." Elizabeth wondered what he might have wished for. A fire truck? A puppy? A father? He'd abandoned the nightly ritual by the time he'd gotten to high school, when she assumed his wishes would have been of a more carnal nature. She smiled as she remembered how he'd set his sights on June McDougal, the neighbor girl—recipient of his first kiss and, as he'd confessed before he joined the Army, his first true love.

Elizabeth shuddered with a darker memory, seeing the desperation in the eyes of June's father as he went door to door, asking about his daughter. She could sympathize with that desperation now, after meeting the uniformed men on her doorstep. She pictured a different set of uniforms visiting June's parents, asking questions of the neighbors, putting up signs. At least she'd been given a body to bury.

Throughout the ordeal, Alex had simply suffered quietly. She remembered the empty coldness in her teenage son's eyes, the stony and pragmatic silence that refused hope. She'd seen his desperation manifest as the stoic determination he'd shown the police and the television news crews. A tightly clutched fist, a clenched jaw, a long sigh of angry frustration. She watched her child, her baby, as he joined the search party, his powerlessness refocused into rage. There was nothing she could do: no meal she could cook, no words she could speak, no magic she could wield. She hadn't looked at him that closely in the months prior to Junie's disappearance, but in the weeks afterward, the child she thought she remembered began to take the silent form of a man. It was no surprise to her when he enlisted. He needed catharsis, she told herself, repeating it like a mantra, calmed by the idea, relaxed by its implications. Charmed, in a way.

She arrived at the condo late in the evening. The wishing star had disappeared in the vague haze of light reflected back from the city. She didn't need the star, though. She had magic of a different kind.

Once inside, she sat at the kitchen table and opened the envelope, spilling its contents out in front of her: a work visa, immigration paperwork, and a Mexican birth certificate for Alessandro Perez—a most uncreative name but the best she could come up with on the spot. At the bottom of the pile lay a laminated identification card with the same name and a picture of her beautiful and handsome son smiling in one corner. The image was from a photo taken just before his second tour, a front portrait of Alex, hair slightly askew, gazing at the camera with amusement. She couldn't remember what he'd been laughing about when she'd snapped the photo, and that lack of memory brought tears to her eyes, which she wiped away with the tips of her fingers. She gathered the papers and dropped them back into the envelope. It was time to set up the altar.

She performed the ritual the same as before, although perhaps with more confidence and a louder voice. When she pulled the *pata* out of its plastic housing she was struck by its acidic and mildewing odor. It left dozens of small hairs behind on the cloth, and she felt her throat close as she considered the possibility that she'd waited too long, delayed the second wish longer than she should have.

Shaking her head to clear it, she sliced her hand and finished out the prayer. She read her prepared statement exactly, feeling the words in her heart as she heard them in her own ears.

Elizabeth's second wish was made.

*****

The number six had its own kind of magic for Elizabeth. She had been taught that the creation of the earth took six days, which was the number of man—and one number away from perfection. It was evenly divisible by both three and two, which enhanced its numerological perfection. Alex had been born in the sixth month. The sum of the letters of his full name was six. And she had last spoken to him six days before the Iraqi's IED blew his body apart.

"I want my son Alex at my door: alive, complete and healthy; the man he was six days before his death," she'd said aloud, completing the second wish. She'd thought it over; done her homework. She worded the wish correctly, she

knew. No rotting corpse would visit her doorstep; no ghost would haunt her dreams at night. The magic would work, she knew in her heart. She'd done everything right. To the letter.

She didn't know how long it would take, so she made a mental checklist of things still left to do. There were boxes to be unpacked, and it was likely he would be hungry when he … arrived. She remembered his complaints about Army food and went into the kitchen to prepare a pancake breakfast for dinner, his favorite meal even as a teenager. She picked up a glass measuring cup and smiled, remembering a toddler Alex gasping in delight as she drew, freehand, animal shapes with the batter. He always ate them with butter only, opting to put syrup on his bacon instead.

There was no bacon. She had forgotten to buy it. She cursed herself aloud for forgetting something so basic, but she couldn't leave now. He could arrive any minute now, confused and hungry and—

A soft knock at the door made her jump. The measuring cup flew out of her hands and bounced across the linoleum, landing surprisingly undamaged beneath the sink. She took it as a sign and swallowed her anxiety, walking purposefully into the living room and up to the front door. Her palm on the door handle was hot on cool, sweaty against the dry metal. The soft knocking sounded again, three raps in quick succession. She stood up straighter, closed her eyes, and turned. The door opened silently inward.

When she unclosed her eyes they focused on a tall bald man, a ball of fur cradled in his arms.

"Did you lose a cat?" he asked. The ball of fur shifted and meowed.

Elizabeth's mouth fell open. The cat meowed again. She shook her head silently, slowly at first, then faster.

"I … no," she said slowly. Then "Hell no, get out." She slammed the door in the man's face, hearing his contemptuous snort and the cat's plaintive meow through the wall. She threaded her fingers into her hair and pulled hard, savoring the pain, experiencing it. Desperate to feel something other than anguish, she backed away from the door and pulled harder. Her eyes watered as the doubt began to manifest. What was she doing? What insanity was this that

she thought a severed monkey paw could —

The knock was louder this time, and more drawn out. Three raps, spaced evenly apart. She dropped her hands and yanked open the door.

"What the hell did I just…" She stopped, her mouth open. Her own eyes stared back at her, confused and amused at the same time: her eyes, in a round olive-skinned face, looking down from a 6-foot 2-inch frame in fatigues and sock feet.

Elizabeth tried to count to ten before exhaling. She got to six before wrapping the man in front of her in her arms, tears welling in her eyes and sobs contained inside her chest. The man hugged her back, releasing her before she was ready, his questioning eyes searching her wet ones for answers.

"Mom?" he asked.

"Yes, darling," she said. "It's Mom."

The tears came, full force, flowing from both of them.

Wish the Third:

Alex ate heartily, as though he hadn't had a good meal in years. Three years, she told herself as she poured more pancake batter. He'd laughed when she served him the first tiny pancakes in vaguely elephant shapes, then politely suggested she save her energy and just make large round ones. He didn't complain about the missing bacon. He ate steadily and she refilled his plate until he belched loudly, apologized, and scooted his chair away from the table. She sat down next to him and smiled, taking in the image of him happy, healthy, and stuffed full of an evening breakfast.

"I'm not sure what to say," he told her, smiling a crooked smile. "I'm a little out of sorts right now."

"You've been through a lot," she said. He frowned and she corrected herself. "I mean it was a long flight. Do you want to have a nap?"

He shook his head. "I know I'm home, but I'm not really sure how I got here," he said, looking around him. "I don't actually remember this place. Did we move?"

She smiled, a warm and loving smile, a mother's smile.

"Yes darling, we moved a few weeks ago." She wanted to avoid specifics, stick to generalities. "Although I haven't actually unpacked everything yet. You know I've wanted out of the city for years, and it's so much cooler up here."

"Got a boyfriend, huh?" he teased. "You're not shacking up with him, I hope."

"Alex!" she scolded playfully.

His expression changed suddenly, confusion furrowing his brow.

"I can't remember Dad."

Elizabeth was taken aback. She never expected she'd have to explain that again.

"Is he dead?" he asked innocently. She nodded. "A plane crash, just before you were born." "So it's just us?" he asked. She smiled.

"Always and—"

"And forever," he finished. "Hey, I need to hit the head. Can I get another pancake?" Elizabeth laughed loudly as they both got up from the table. He was back. Her boy was really back. Healthy, happy, and as charming as ever. For the first time since the paw had been in her possession did she allow herself to relax, ever so slightly, as the batter steamed on the stove.

"Thing is, Mom, I don't really remember a lot of stuff," he said as he returned and flopped back into his chair. His hair was rumpled. "I got hair, so I don't guess I got shot in the brain, did I?"

"No darling, you weren't shot, but we can talk about that later. We can talk about everything later." She flipped the pancake onto a plate and brought it to him. He rolled it into a straw shape and bit off half.

"It's okay if you got a boyfriend," he told her. "I hate to think of you being all alone."

"I'm not alone." She sat down next to him and patted his knee. "I have you."

"You know what I mean. Carly used to talk about how much she wished her dad would get remarried."

"Carly?"

"Oh yeah, I forgot. I was gonna tell you about her, eventually." He looked down at his plate and pushed what remained of the pancake around in a circle. "Thing is, we're not supposed to fraternize, you know? But Carly and I— well, she liked the same things as me, and she was about the only person to understand my jokes. We kind of hung out together cause you can't really go on a date over there, you know?" Elizabeth nodded. "I'm jealous," she teased.

His expression hardened. "Don't be. She got stabbed in the throat by a street vendor selling coffee. I shot him myself. In the gut so he took a while to die. It was the least I could do for her."

Elizabeth brought her hand to her mouth.

"I'm … I'm so sorry, darling. I'm sorry you had to go through that." She wanted to reach out to him, to stroke his hair back over his ear the way she'd done in his childhood, but his clenched jaw warned her away.

"You know if you watch the eyes you can tell the exact moment when they die. It's wild."

The voice was casual, almost childlike, but the eyes that looked at her were not a child's eyes. They were a man's. A soldier's, she reassured herself. And sometimes soldiers did unpleasant things. The eyes flicked away and she settled herself with the knowledge that he was here now, where he wouldn't have to be a soldier anymore. He could be a regular young man with girlfriends and a muscle car, and he would join his mother in church on Sundays, and they would meet on the beach once a month for a shrimp boil. She had it all worked out already. Figured out all the details.

"Thing is, I'm kinda tired, Mom," he said. "You mind if I just maybe hit the sack early? We can catch up in the morning, if that's okay."

"Of course it's okay," she told him, but inside her chest, her heart was breaking. She wanted to savor the sight of him, listen to him talk, feed him—take care of him, her beautiful baby boy. She gathered her strength and smiled. "Your room is just down the hall. I haven't unpacked your clothes yet. There are fresh PJs on the bed, though." She narrowed her eyes to prevent the tears from flowing, pretending she was sizing him up. "I bought different sizes because I wasn't sure."

"That's cool. Thanks." They stood up together and he embraced her. She wrapped her arms around him, pulling him closer to her, smelling his slightly unwashed scent with pleasure. He was warm and alive, a steady heartbeat in his chest and rhythmic breaths flowing through his lungs.

Alex released her and burped loudly.

"Sorry. Not bad manners, just good cookin', right?"

She returned his smile and took the used dishes to the sink as he headed down the hallway. A minute later she heard the water running, and only then did she pour herself a glass of whiskey and have a seat at the table. She stayed there until she heard the water shut off and the soft thudding of his feet on the floor. She waited half an hour before venturing out of the kitchen and down the hall to the bathroom, where she found his abandoned fatigues on the floor. She wanted to take them out and burn them, but she rolled them up and took them to the laundry room.

The bundle was heavier than she expected, and as she went through the multitude of pockets she found papers, keys, a wallet, his cell phone, a wad of foreign paper money, and some assorted change. She dropped the items in a basket, but fished out the phone. It was the same model she still carried, purchased at the same time as her own. She'd never needed to upgrade since Alex was the only person she'd wanted to call or text. The phone was dead. She took it back in the kitchen and plugged it into her charger.

Only when she heard him snoring did she venture down the hallway to her bedroom, retrieve the little box, and return to the kitchen for the final ritual. As she set up the items, she couldn't help but notice the sorry state of the *pata*. It was nearly hairless now, and covered in a fuzzy mold that seemed to have eaten away at the petrified flesh underneath. It was at least half as small as when she'd first bought it, and something made her feel the magic it contained wouldn't survive much longer. But she was ready.

As she lit the candles, she rehearsed her final request. In the stories, this was where the magic went wrong and cursed the magician, or where he failed to say the right words and all he'd accomplished was destroyed. As she dripped the transubstantiated blood onto the *pata*, it cracked. When she drew the knife across her palm and the drops impacted the dried paw, they dissolved what little was left of it, scattering hairs and bits of dried bone and skin in the little bowl. A candle hissed as a bubble in the wax burst and sent liquid into the flame.

"I wish," she rehearsed in her mind, "for my son to live a long and healthy life, free from physical and mental disease, safe from accident or injury until his 96th birthday, whereupon the normal rules of life and death will apply." Six again, in nine plus six, added together, and 96 was certainly old enough to enjoy one's children, grandchildren, and possibly even great-grandchildren.

When the sun finally dropped below the horizon and the first star became visible in her picture window, she spoke the words aloud.

Elizabeth made her third and final wish.

***

"Has it really been three years?" Alex asked after a yawn.

In the morning light his face was blank; she couldn't read him. She poured him another cup of coffee before answering.

"You were missing for a while, then in the hospital for a little while longer. I don't really know all the details," she said quickly. "But there was a death certificate issued, which means they had to get you a new social security number and I know this is going to sound ridiculous, but I had them make a new name for you." It all came out in a rush, sounding rehearsed and false, even to her ears, but she stood by it. "I thought you might want a fresh start, after all … I mean after everything…"

He watched her a long time before responding. His eyes searched her face, and she found herself blushing. He knew she was lying. That iron gaze saw right though her. She hid the lies from him, looking away, out the window at the ocean rolling gently below. A sandpiper picked apart a small crab on the beach, deftly avoiding each of its spindly legs.

"After all that has transpired," she said quietly.

She heard his chair slide on the floor. He knelt beside her, took her hand in his, and rested his forehead against hers.

"A fresh start sounds great," he whispered. "Thing is, I don't think I was really Army material anyway. They would have axed me eventually. At least now I can work on engines and stuff. I was thinking of hanging around here and being a boat mechanic. I mean if you'll let me crash on your couch for a few."

She smiled. "I assumed you would. Take your time getting readjusted, darling. No hurry. I've missed having you around. No need to look for your own place just yet." She raised her hand to her hair and brushed it out of her eyes.

"Did you hurt yourself?" he asked, nodding at the bandage on her palm.

"Oh," she said, feeling silly and relieved. "The knife slipped while I was cutting an apple. Let that be a lesson to you—always cut away from you."

He drained the last of his coffee. "I think I could use a little fresh air."

She smiled. "I'd love a walk."

He shook his head. "I'm sorry I meant, alone. I just need a little time by myself. Soul-search, clear my head kind of thing. You understand."

She didn't, but nodded, biting the inside of her lip to keep her emotions under control.

"He's a pistol," she remembered telling her friends when a toddler Alex ran circles around her. He had always been a headstrong boy, fiercely independent and keeping mostly to himself in the grammar school years, but the teenage Alex had seemed to enjoy spending time with her, often foregoing friends to stay home and watch old movies with his mother. Now he was distancing himself again. Already. He hadn't even been back 48 hours.

After he left she realized she'd forgotten to return his phone. Fully charged, it sat on the counter. She powered it on, smiling when she saw the wallpaper photo—a pretty redhead in camouflage, looking sideways, as though she wasn't aware of the camera. The girlfriend? Elizabeth sniffed. Her phone's wallpaper was still his boot camp graduation photo. A boy was always his mother's baby, but a mother was quickly replaced in the boy's heart by his woman.

The photo made her wary. She'd deactivated the phone three years ago, after the week she'd sent dozens of messages that had gone unanswered. After the notification officers arrived. After she tried and largely failed to "move on." She assumed the phone's memory would have been erased when the service was cancelled, but the wallpaper photograph indicated otherwise. She couldn't leave a record of her last dozen desperate calls to him. She found the menu and scrolled through the phone's options.

The call log was blank. The sent messages folder was empty, but the list of incoming text messages was enormous. She clicked on the most recently received, following the onesided conversation back to the summer before Alex had been killed. As she reached the oldest entries, she went back down through them, reading them again in chronological order.

The messages themselves made no sense. Most were from the same number, listed in his contacts as simply "C." The older notes gradually switched from simple one- or twoword answers to longer messages, and then back to short ones again. *"No,"* and *"Go Away,"* were repeated, over and over. *"Leave me alone,"* with varying amounts of exclamation marks was a favorite. Why had he kept these? She read the longer messages aloud. The grammar was poor but the sentiment was hard to misunderstand.

"Stop calling me," read an early text. *"Im serious leave me alone,"* read another. The messages grew longer, the language more desperate. *"If u dont stop I will inform the CO"* preceded *"I told u leave me alone I have tried to be nice to u but I am reporting this."*

The last message from C was the most disturbing, dated just three days before her son's death: *"WTF???!!! I told u to*
leave me alone. I know its u out there. Leave. Now."

She dropped the phone and it clattered on the linoleum floor, separating at the seams. Slowly she got up from the table, picked up the broken pieces, and went into the laundry alcove. She dropped the phone's remains in the basket and retrieved the folded papers she'd pulled from his pocket. A torn scrap of newspaper described the disappearance of a Corporal Carleen Duggan from her unit in Mosul. There wasn't much information in the article, but the accompanying photo made Elizabeth sick to her stomach. The missing girl had the same face as her son's wallpaper photograph.

The newspaper fluttered from her hand.

"Not again," she said quietly.

***

She heard him open the front door. He called out to her, but she couldn't make herself answer.

"Mom?" he asked again from the door frame. "What are you doing?"

The floor of the second bedroom was covered with clothes, books and memorabilia from Alex's school days. Empty storage boxes had been thrown on the bed, their contents dumped on the rug. She sat with her back to him. When she didn't respond, he came up behind her and knelt down by her side.

"What is all this, Alex?" she asked in a calm voice. In front of her on the rug were dozens of close-up pictures of a smiling blonde girl wearing a gold locket around her neck— June McDougal, her son's high-school sweetheart. Her open letters lay scattered, showing the same large, loopy handwriting demanding the receiver to *"leave her alone,"* and *"go away,"* and more dramatically, *"burn in hell."* The letters were all addressed to the same name.

Alex sighed.

"And who the hell are *they?*" She gestured to a stack of Polaroids that captured a half dozen different women, greeneyed and blonde-haired. Newspaper clippings accompanied the photos, each one relating the same "missing woman" storyline.

"You went through my stuff." It was more of an observation than a question.

"I kept all this in storage for you." She didn't turn to look at him, but picked up a small velvet box containing two rings, a bracelet, a watch, and a gold locket. She took the locket and pried it apart to reveal two antique photographs. "These are Junie's grandparents," she said. "The locket was her grandmother's and she wore it all the time, the paper said. She was wearing it when she went missing. I remember the posters."

"I wanted to keep something to remember her, Mom." His voice was soft in her ear, imploring. He touched her shoulder but she shrugged his hand away.

"These weren't enough?" she snarled at him, snatching up another box. She opened it and let the contents drop to the rug, scattering seven short white objects.

"Just rocks," he said casually.

"Phalanges, Alex. I was a nurse for thirty years. I recognize finger bones."

He sighed and dropped down on the floor next to her. He rummaged in his pocket and pulled out another white object, this one looked sticky, still tinged a dark red on the ends. It smelled coppery and earthy. He sniffed it briefly before tossing it in the pile with the others.

"It's not your fault, you know," he told her. "I hope you don't start thinking that or anything." He brushed her hair back from her ear before resting his palm on her shoulder. "Thing is, I sorta thought I was done with all that. Carly was gonna be the last one. It kinda stopped being fun for a while, you know, with all the shit going on over there in Iraq. And then I got blew up, and I'm back here, and well, everything changed."

"I brought you back," she said, her voice wavering.

"Yeah, I kinda figured that out already." He patted her shoulder gently. "You're a good Mom, always self-sacrificing and stuff. We're a good team: you and me, always and forever, just like when I was a kid, right?"

Elizabeth was silent. The hand on her shoulder was warm, but not warm enough to remove the chill. He inched closer to her, resting his thigh against hers. She started to scoot away, but he dropped his hand on her leg and kept her in place.

Elizabeth shook her head slowly. "I brought you back." Warm tears welled in her eyes. "I did everything right. Down to the letter."

"I know." He leaned his head to rest on her shoulder. This time she didn't pull away. "And for the right reasons, too. I don't blame you or anything. You were a really great Mom. It's not like you messed me up as a kid and made me do this," he said, motioning to the mess in front of them.

The tears flowed now, but not for the pile of shattered lives on the floor. Not for the undoubtedly beautiful blonde whose picture would soon appear on the evening news, and not for all the other women who would cross his path over the next seventy-something years. These tears Elizabeth shed for herself and her son, always and forever.

"Don't cry, Mom." He reached his other arm around her shoulder to hug her. "You didn't know what I was when you did ... whatever you did to bring me back."

In his voice she could hear a tinier, higher-pitched voice calling her "Mommy," and the mewing soft cries of hunger when he'd failed to latch onto her breast properly and she'd had to squeeze out drops of milk into a syringe to feed him. Heard him laughing with her at Saturday cartoons, and negotiating with her over his curfew. She heard his last message to her, three years before her heart had become so empty she thought she might have swallowed her own soul from grief. She heard him softly repeating his comforting mantra: "you didn't know" in her ear as he held her, the warmth of his living skin cool against her burning cheeks.

"Oh, Alex," she whispered as the tears fell. "But I did."

About the Author

Amanda Hard is a former journalist and magazine editor currently pursuing an MFA in Creative Writing (Fiction) at Murray State University in Kentucky. Her horror fiction has appeared in numerous magazines and print anthologies and her flash fiction has been featured in three graphic collections from The Daily Nightmare. She is a member of the Horror Writers Association and lives in the cornfields of southern Indiana with her husband, son, two dogs, and enough unattached dog hair to knit a third one.

Pint Bottle Press
99¢
DOUBLE-BARREL HORROR
ONE DIRT ROAD
Last Clown Out
K. TRAP JONES

One Dirt Road

by K. Trap Jones

Every town has one. Each resident has heard the folklore embedded within generations. Children grow up with the rumors, and adults question the reasoning, but somewhere on the jagged line between myth and reality dwells the truth. Twisted and morphed between friends; altered with each spoken story regarding that one dirt road on the outskirt of town leading to unknown places; speaking of irrational terrors.

Growing up in a small northern Florida town, I was well aware of such a road leading deep into an area of dense woods. Rumors were numerous with regard to what dwelled at the end. Some told tales of troubled witches who would feast upon those who trespassed while others spoke of mass graves used to house those who died from an ancient plague. Every night the souls would rise, searching for new bodies to possess.

As a young kid, my friends and I would venture to the road with backpacks filled with drinks and snacks. The whole way there was filled with bravery and excitement, but our attitudes diminished once our tattered shoes landed on the dirt of the infamous road. Silence suffocated the bravery; fear reduced the excitement. I could barely swallow as I gazed toward the bend where the dirt met the shadows of the trees.

The newspapers told the stories of every missing person in town. There was one thing in common. They were all last seen in the vicinity of the road. The swaying trees along with the gawks from the crows added to the eerie atmosphere.

Overgrown vines and bushes fed on the numerous *No Trespassing* signs.

Standing at the beginning of the road, we proceeded with the ritualistic game. Four different colored stones were placed into a bag. A quick shake made sure the odds were fair. We were all terrified of the darkened unlucky stone, but like all dares, someone had to lose. Sweating profusely, we hid our shivering well.

There were four of us equating to a twenty-five percent chance for disaster. Andy went first and opened his palm to reveal a light colored stone. He gasped for breath then changed his attitude from scared to brave. Paul chose another light colored stone. My pain percentage immediately doubled.

I tried to peer into the bag with hopes to see some sort of coloring, but the shadows concealed the stones perfectly. My palms were wet and cold; my fingers curled backwards as if to protest. I felt the two stones at the bottom. One was life, one was death, and they both handled the same. I made a decision and pulled out my clenched fist. Everyone was eager to see, especially Matt who was next. I held his fate within my palm as well.

With a trembling wrist, I opened my hand revealing the darkened stone. I momentarily died as my heart was desperately ripped from my chest by a passing crow. I was drunk with fear and blurred vision, hoping I would awaken within the comfort of my bed. Much like my choice in stones, I would not be so lucky.

A rotation of my shoulder allowed the backpack to fall to the dirt. A swipe of my hand cleared the nervous sweat from my eyes. We always prepared letters, much like soldiers in war, to be given to our parents if we didn't return. I handed mine to Andy before walking down the road. A few feet in, I passed the old rusty beer cans, rumored to belong to partying teenagers before the witches attacked. The wind whistled across the open containers emitting a sound mimicking screams from the dead.

On the left were the broken arrows embedded in the trees where the cannibal cult staked their victims before feasting on them alive. Some say it still reeks of burnt flesh. I could see the bend in the road just up ahead. It was no big task to reach it; I could still see my friends. The sight of them offered a small piece of safety even though I could never outrun the flying witches and convicts.

Of all the distractions, the trees were the worst. They seemed to taunt me with irregular movements and shadows. The sounds of the branches bending toyed with my emotions, but I proceeded. My goal was to reach the bend and go just beyond it. I had no intention of making it to the end, as I enjoyed living. I stood at the threshold of the bend and after one quick glance back to my friends, I walked further.

A darkened stretch of road came into view, even more terrifying than the first. The trees bent around forming a natural tunnel concealing the sun. Dare or no dare, I decided to make haste and hightail it back. There was no disappointment or teasing with regard to the dare, only acceptance of the fact I made it around the bend and was still breathing.

Ten years later, after going away to college and studying law, I found myself back in my childhood town. I opened a law office not far from my original home. Not a lot had changed through the years, and to my surprise the rumors of the dirt road still existed. The tales altered a bit, but the basis was still the same.

My curiosity once again peaked as I found myself at the beginning of the dirt road while jogging. I had time to spare, so I walked down the road. I'll admit it; I did hesitate as the memories of my youth bombarded my visions. There was no one waiting for my return. I was alone, being guided by the demented tales.

Maturity allowed me to overcome the witches and demons, but the convicts were a little more believable. However, the odds of them still remaining in the area seemed unlikely. I reached the bend and thought nothing of it. The infamous bend in the road … I stood at the crossroads that separated boys from men. It felt like a relief of sorts, to conquer those crazy tales I dwelled upon as a child.

Through the tunnel of trees I went. I had never ventured as far. There were several rusty signs scattered about and broken-down cars devoured by vines. It became an adrenaline rush to disprove all the rumors. I wanted nothing more than to find the end at a riverbank or an overgrown field.

The road led further into the trees where I discovered a small house. The windows were boarded up and the surrounding vegetation had been left to grow freely. I proceeded up the porch steps and knocked on the front door without any fear. To my surprise, the wooden door creaked open to reveal an elderly man with glasses.

"I don't want any," he said with a scowl.

"No, I'm not selling anything. I was just jogging."

"Jogging, eh? I don't get too many people down the road here. I was just fetching some water, would you like some?" he said, widening the door.

"Yes, that's very kind of you." I said, stepping through the door.

The house was well put together inside with pictures of his family hanging on the wall and an old time television with antenna. I sat on the couch while he brought a glass of water.

"You know the meat factory?" he said, handing me the glass.

"Yeah, the smoke stacks are literally a historical landmark in town."

"Generations of my family have worked there. I'm the Meat Manager."

I knew the factory well, as I used to go there on field trips in school. He appeared humbled and certainly not a witch, demon or convict.

"You must hear the rumors about the road?" I said out of curiosity.

"Ah yes, I pay no attention to them. I never use the front road. I travel to the factory from behind the house. I don't mind, I keep to myself."

There was something odd about the man. His leg never stopped shaking as he sat on the edge of the chair.

"I didn't even know there was a back road to the factory."

"Been there for as long as I can remember."

His anxious behavior made him appear eager for me to leave. I did not want to overstay my visit, so after drinking the water I stood and handed him the glass.

"Thank you so much for your hospitality, but I must be getting back."

"Yes, the sun will be setting soon," he announced, quickly standing.

I turned to the door, which had no knob or handle. A small mirror hung on the left side. In the reflection, I remember seeing the old man swinging a hammer. Time seemed to slow as I saw the glare from his glasses and the shine of the metal tip. I do not remember the impact nor did I feel the pain.

My vision slowly faded in and out until the blurriness vanished. Bright lights passed overhead. I remember them well because I could not close my eyelids to shield against the brightness. Pain introduced itself in various portions of my body. I could not turn my head as my neck was being held tightly in a device that kept me looking straight. Held open by sharpened objects, my eyelids were tearing under the pressure of wanting to blink. Through fear unlike any other, I was being wheeled on a cart down a long hallway. My ankles and wrists were shackled and pulled downward on either side, causing a terrible pain within the shoulders and thighs. I could see the chin of the Meat Manager and the glare from his glasses as I unwillingly stared up. Small quick breaths of torment were all I could muster.

"Ah, you're awake. The tour is about to begin," he said with a smile.

The wobbly wheels of the cart halted. He shifted my skull to the right with the turn of a handle protruding from the contraption.

"I know the rumors, all of which are untrue. Witches and demons; the imagination never ceases to amaze. Everyone wants to know, but fear always gets in the way. Then there are those who tempt fate, denying the human sanctity of safety. Risk-takers, rolling the dice with life. For me, there is but a fine line between bravery and stupidity."

He pushed me further before stopping, twisting my head to the left. I wanted to shut my eyes, but couldn't.

"This is the Carving Room. Nobody likes fatty meat. It's quite the undertaking to trim human flesh; a lost art form if you ask me."

Large meat hooks dangled from the ceiling, holding the butchered remains of corpses. My throat convulsed as bile spilled over my tongue.

"Get it all out. I can't have you contaminate anything. Cleanliness is godliness. Wait, I jumped the gun. I do apology as I was not thinking straight."

He forcefully rotated the handle, twisting my head to the right.

"The Drain is the first stop before the Carving Room. I feel so absent-minded. One cannot carve unless all of the blood is removed first." He patted my head.

A large drain resided in the center of the concaved floor. Tears swelled in my eyes as I saw lifeless cadavers hanging upside down with their necks cut. The floor was covered in a sludge of blood that slowly dripped down the clogged drain. As the wheels went forward, he provided another forceful rotation of the handle where I involuntarily looked through the doorway of the next room.

"This here is my favorite–the Chopshop. This is where the true talent of a butcher shines. The cuts, the filets, the ounces."

Butchered corpses lined the entranceway, leading to a lone table in the middle. Blood-stained knives of all sizes hung against the wall.

"Pardon the mess. I was preparing an order when you knocked," he explained, pushing the cart forward.

The squeaky wheels carried me onward until we reached another room. The handle rotated and so did my head.

"The Grinder. Ground beef perfection. Due to government standards and the different ratio in fat content, human flesh needs to be folded in. Ground chuck receives the least amount due to its low price and typical 15- to 20-percent fat content. As the prices go up, the more flesh additive is introduced. Ground round is next then sirloin. I would say I deliver a batch of meat weekly to be filtered in with the typical cow before the packaging and delivery to the stores."

He wheeled me next to a window and rotated the device.

"You see the food store? It's a bit of a distance, but if you squint hard enough, you can make it out." He rested his elbow on my ear. "It should calm you to know that no part of you will go to waste."

I was beyond fear; I felt no pain. The only emotion remaining was sadness. The ceiling spun around as the cart turned, and he wheeled me back to the beginning. Staring upward, I saw the top of the doorway. I could feel the relief of pain as he released my legs and arms. After detaching my eyelids and head, my body slid off the cart into the sludge of the Drain room floor.

A swinging light bulb provided the only light. I heard him sharpening a knife, but could not tell where he was due to my blurring vision. He grabbed my leg and pulled me to the center of the room before kneeling down atop of me. Light glared off his glasses, and his tongue brushed against his teeth. The blade indented into my neck as he grabbed my hair.

Adrenaline prompted me to act. I snatched the back of his head-and slammed his face into my forehead. His nose collapsed under the force and his glasses released the lenses. Dropping the knife, he scurried away as I quickly crawled through the sludge toward the hallway.

"Fuck! You broke my glasses!" he screamed as I slid myself into the Grinder room and hid behind the machine.

Within moments, he was scouring the hallway looking for me. Hidden within the shadows, I watched as he stumbled into the room, squinting to see. Even though he held two cleavers, I felt more powerful than him. Creeping within the darkness, I waited for his back to turn before pushing him into the wall. With two handfuls of hair, I slammed his head against the brick, forcing him to drop the knives.

Coughing up blood, he slouched to the ground as I stood above him with his knives in my hands. I shredded his chest and arms as he tried to block the attack. With one last effort, he lunged at me. I sliced one knife into his stomach and the other into his upper chest.

His muscles twitched as his lungs wheezed for air. I pulled him over to the Grinder. The rattling machine sputtered and powered up with a flick of the main switch. With no remorse, I shoved his head deep into the metal teeth. His muffled screams became muted as the top portion of his scalp ground into blood, hair and bone, allowing his headless corpse to fall back to the floor.

The outside air never felt so good flowing through my lungs. Stumbling down the road I went through the tunnel of trees, nearing the bend. As I turned, I saw people standing at the beginning of the road. As soon as they noticed a man all covered in blood, they immediately ran. I passed the charred tree and the broken arrows as I left the dirt road.

Life went on, and I still practice law in the same town, but I never forgot what happened that day. The Meat

Manager's house was demolished and the factory has since closed, but the nightmares still continue. Even today as I sit in the local diner waiting for my vegetarian hamburger, others still spread rumors about what lies at the end of the dirt road.

Last Clown Out

by K. Trap Jones

Pain and suffering was not what I envisioned when I first sought employment at the circus. I never could've anticipated the mental abuse. It was far from the cotton candy and soda binges I thought it would be. Instead, I find myself sitting in a smoke-filled trailer overlooking a wall of empty whiskey bottles, conjuring a plan to escape the torment once and for all. The red and blue lights of the police pierce through the window, illuminating the inside like a demented Christmas tree. The annoying man behind the megaphone tries desperately to calm my nerves, providing assurance that no harm will come to me. A damn, tiny car—the reason I find myself in this situation; the reason why this gun will not leave my hand.

Torment; a bloody cesspool of an experience with the ability to alter even the happiest of occasions. Unforgiving, seeking out those who are emotionally weakened, but I was not weak. My mind was sharp and precise in the intentions guiding my career choice. However, my size characterized me when I first stepped foot on the circus grounds. Height was not a gift given to me, but I never gave a shit about what others thought. I sought solitude within the clown posse; the misfits of the circus trade. There was a group of us who performed each night. We were a team; an elite gathering of entertainers attracting a wide audience within our little section of the circus grounds.

Everything changed with the introduction of the car. One little car; one insane idea from the minds of management set in motion the beginning of the end. The deranged concept was to stuff all six of us in there while the audience sat gapemouthed in amazement as we exited. They assured each of us the new routine would be a crowd favorite and indeed it was, but the time spent in the spotlight would soon fade. Due to my size, I was the first clown in and the last clown out. All of my previous time spent in front of the audience and part of the team was altered. I was forced to trade my once-cherished spotlight for waiting inside a cramped, fucking car.

My audience time was reduced down to nothing. I tried to transfer to a different area of the circus, but the crowd adored the shock factor of a small clown jumping out of the car just when they thought no one else was in there. I hated the car with a passion. Just touching the door handle tied my stomach into knots, plaguing my emotions. Ducking my head under and sliding to the far edge provided me with an overwhelming sense of despair. Feeling the weight of the car shift with every clown gifted my gut with motion sickness. I was never claustrophobic, but I quickly became a victim. There was no air; there was no room. The distance the car traveled from behind the fence to where we exited was not long, but it felt like clocking miles on the devil's highway.

I hated everything about my time in the car. My face was often smashed against the window with the arm rest securely puncturing my ribcage. My spine was forced to contort so I could fit in my designated space. I abhorred the second clown who was crammed beside me. His bony knees always resided deep in my spine.

The car was remote-controlled and, to our misfortune, led by a less than punctual operator. Often times, he forgot to change the batteries in the controller and the damn thing would die on us. During those situations, our tempers and patience were tested. We were not the happy-go-lucky clowns the audience expected us to be. We were a time bomb set to explode. We despised each other and even concocted schemes to reduce the amount of clowns on our team for the sole purpose of gaining an inch more room within the car. We would hear the audience laugh as they looked upon the small vehicle rocking back and forth, our muffled voices leaking through the glass. Underneath the humor and applause, there were death threats and short jabs thrown to the mid-section. It was a pressure cooker of emotions ready to ignite.

As we reached the peak of our internal anger, the grinding wheels of the car carried us forward into the spotlight, magnifying the heat and transporting us into a virtual sweatshop. With my face plastered against the window, the smolder from the spotlight became unbearable. The white paint caked upon my face melted. With my hands pinned against the door and underneath the second clown, I could offer no relief to my watering eyes. When the door finally opened and gifted us with an exit, we altered our evil expressions to one of smiles and glee. The whole process became a pattern which always concluded the same; a vision of a cruel demise delivered to the other clowns.

The amount of time I spent in the car was unmatched by any of the others. There were a total of six in the car and to be the first one in and the last one out, pretty much sucked. I couldn't sleep at night due to the ghoulish visions of the beast. My mind was relentless, morphing it into an oven where I was cooked alive. It was a nightly occurrence, leaving me exhausted when the sun rose from behind the carousel.

Each one of us within the demented clown team had their own degree of sanity. We never knew which one of us would snap on any given day. We drank heavily before each event, even prior to the crowd arrival. We often prayed no one would show up, sparing us from the death mobile. However, the constant promotion and the high flying banners of the mystical clown car always sent annoying spectators our way. With the over-produced theme song blaring from one barely functional speaker, the six of us took one more shot and snuffed out cigarettes. The grinding of the door hinges always made a brief spark, causing my lip to snarl in disgust. I often closed my eyes as I entered, trying my best to avoid the vision of the stained seat cushion.

The last clown in was the biggest, and I swear to God he grew in size every day. I watched his large belly expand as he shoved all the circus shit foods like corndogs and funnel cakes down his gullet. Maybe it was my mind playing tricks on me, but I felt my small space in the car decreasing on a daily basis due to his excessive eating. I hated him with a passion not only for his appetite, but also for the fact he would always take one more drag of his cigarette before entering the car, exhaling after he shut the damn door. Not only did we not have enough air to support us all, but he lessened it with his greedy puff of smoke.

Don't get me wrong, I hated each one of the clowns equally. Clown Two always tested the limits of my patience by inching over. Clown Three could never hold his liquor and gave new meaning to the term *bladder bust*. Clown Four was the smelliest prick I had ever met. Clown Five would pass out almost every time, and we would have to kick him to get out of the car. Clown One was the large bastard I wanted to butcher into little pieces and feed him to the elephants.

On one particular summer night during the circus stay in San Antonio, we were taking our traditional shots while swatting away mosquitoes. The weather was brutal and unforgiving with a dry heat that would make Hades question his realm of choice. The makeup smeared across our faces.

The attached noses were barely hanging on, and the red hair itched like an unwashed ball sack. With sweat dripping down my thighs, I stared in disbelief at the steam rising from the metal exterior of the car. I didn't want to get into the toaster again. I couldn't go through the pattern anymore. As the theme song played, I panicked. My stomach tightened and I puked all over Clown Two's big red shoes.

Clown Four opened the car door, causing the spark from the hinges, and I could feel the heat pouring out. My eyes watered and halted my momentum. I couldn't do it; I didn't want to enter the car again. Clown One grabbed the back of my neck, pushing me forward to where I barely was able to duck under the roof. My face met with the interior heat, immediately liquefying whatever I had left of the red paint surrounding my mouth. I felt Clown Two on my backside, so I slid over into my space. With my face pressed against the window, the hot glass blistered my cheek.

The wheels grinded forward, but it wasn't the usual distance. It came to a stop. With one eye, I could see the operator screwing around with the controller. He tried new batteries and even banged the controller against his leg, but nothing worked. Clown Three twisted his neck for a perfect view out the back window. With whiskey-slurred speech, he detailed someone pushing us into position. Once there, Clown One tried to open the door, but it was fucking stuck.

The operator came over and tried from the outside, but nothing. All of us yelled to Clown One to open the damn door, but nothing worked. Within seconds, panic set in and the realization we were trapped instantly turned everyone against one another. Fists were thrown blindly wherever there was enough room to do so. We pinched, twisted and grabbed at any area of flesh regardless of where it was. Wigs were removed, outfits were torn and our white faces became stained with blood.

Our energy faded as the heat consumed our souls. We were bloody and bruised when the operator finally managed to unseal the door. Clown One immediately fell out followed by Clown Two. The rest of us had to be pulled from the metal casket. The crowd stood in silence as all the children wept at the sight of six bloody and beaten clowns laid out upon the ground, gasping for breath. If any of us had an ounce of energy left, we would have spent it on dismembering the operator. Instead, we just laid there while the mosquitoes feasted upon our open wounds.

We were given a reprieve from the event, but it was not for us to heal; it was to allow time for the car to be fixed. During the downtime, we all continued to drink heavily as we knew eventually the pit of death would ride again. Our hatred for one another only increased. We were forced to sell balloons to the patrons during the downtime. When any two clowns roamed near one another, a verbal assault erupted. I tried to keep my distance, but it was inevitable that paths would cross.

I remember coming across Clown Four, and it got ugly real quick. He tripped me causing the cluster of balloons to float away. He made a comment regarding my height and how I would never be able to reach them. I lost my shit and jumped to his chest, gripping his neck with my fingers. I squeezed until I felt the inner workings of his throat. I heard the screams of the crowd, but I only focused on ripping the spine from his corpse. I turned slightly just in time to see a large red clown boot coming my way. The force sent me flying into a nearby cotton candy machine. I stumbled to get up, but I could see Clown Two kicking the other one still on the ground. Clown Five came out of nowhere and knocked out Clown Four with a trash scooper.

I thought things couldn't get any worse until the announcement about the fixed car. Hearing those words forced vomit to creep up, coating my tongue. I spent the whole day leading up to the event drowning my sorrows within a sea of whiskey, hoping the ship would sink and bury my carcass within the deepest trench. Instead, I devised a sinister plan to not only take out the car, but also Clowns One through Five. The whiskey made the plan perfect in every way. It appeared foolproof, but I was also seeing two of everything.

To begin, I visited the operator who was putting oil in the car. I needed a short time alone with the vehicle, so I told him management needed to see him regarding a loose bolt on the merry-go-round. He took the bait, leaving me behind. With an ice pick, I chiseled out a small hole in the window where my face usually resided and then hid a small canister of propane where my feet would be. A section of black carpet concealed the tank well within the natural shadows of the car. After making sure the door did in fact work, I quickly left and awaited for the event to take place.

The sun sank behind the bungee slingshot attraction, and the neon lights of the circus provided color to the darkened sky. Cigarettes and whiskey filled our lungs and stomach. The sheer dread of entering the car tattooed each one of their faces, but not mine. I was the only clown smiling, and it wasn't because of the makeup. I envisioned the events through my drunken mind. The fuzz of the speakers bled the beginning notes of the theme song, prompting everyone to snuff out cigarettes and gulp down one more shot. They all looked to the car with disgust. I saw it as an end of an era.

Clown Five grabbed the door handle, producing the spark from the hinges. The stained cushion welcomed my hand as I crept inside. In preparation for the squeeze effect, I positioned my mouth against the hole in the window, making sure my right arm extended down to reach the nozzle of the propane tank. One by one, the other clowns forced their way in.

Clown One shut the door, releasing his typical smoke cloud. As sweat rolled, I heard the music from the outside as the operator forced the wheels of the car to advance. With a hand on the nozzle, I opened the valve of the tank. The sweat from my fingers made the grip slippery. I heard small amounts of the gas exiting, but it wasn't enough. From the sound of the music, I didn't have much time. With words of discomfort from the mouth of Clown Five, I shifted a shoulder allowing for my arm to sink further down. With a better grip, I rotated the valve fully open. The humming of the gas spilled into the car at a quick pace.

Suctioning my lips around the hole in the window, I tried to slow my breathing as to not panic. The clean air siphoned into my lungs as the others coughed. I kept my mouth sealed to the hole as I felt the others struggling, pushing from behind. I closed my eyes and focused on the Texas air as I heard the others vomit and spit. The gas burnt my exposed skin as I heard Clown One fiddling for the door handle. It was time to escape. I took a deep breath of clean air and pulled away from the window. With all five of the other clowns fruitlessly pushing towards the opposite door, I opened mine and immediately fell out.

My feet provided leverage to shut the door, but the arm of Clown Five reached out, wedged between the metal. I kicked at the door until he could no longer endure the pain and retracted his arm. The door was closed with one final push as Clown One, on the other side, grabbed his handle and twisted. The metal hinges grinded against one another, producing the small spark, igniting the gas and exploding the car.

The audience sat in awe as bits of clown flesh and bright synthetic wigs rained down upon them. My door collided with me during the explosion, breaking both my nose and jaw. When my eyes became focused, I could vaguely see everyone coated in red.

I sat up slowly in a huge puddle of blood. Melted red clown shoes and severed arms littered the ground. The clown carcasses were tossed a great distance and skewered with bits of the metal car. The stained cushion had blown to the other side of the crowd, still ablaze.

The audience did not know how to respond. Some were frozen in place while others ran hysterically.

The paramedics arrived and from the looks on their faces, they didn't have a clue where to begin. Once they made eye contact with me, they rushed over with their boots sloshing in the makeshift lake of blood. I was put on a stretcher and taken away from the scene.

A week later, as I lay battered and bruised from the incident, I could tell something was awry. A suspicious wind blew through the Texas night, whispering a demented tale. After the incident, I received visitors wishing a speedy recovery, but like all lies, it slowly died off. My last visitor was the Bearded Lady who reluctantly informed me of an ongoing investigation. She said the entire circus staff was being questioned. She offered no further information and quickly left. The next night, I saw the police snooping around outside my trailer.

As the moon surfaces, I still remain within the trailer, even as the police realize the situation was no accident. They beg me to turn myself in, but empty whiskey bottles tempt me with a different outcome; one that will lead me to salvation, far away from this cursed land of neon lights and fried food. It is a solution which grants me the freedom from the sadistic environment. No more clowns, no small cars, no balloons.

I can sense the cops on my doorstep. One bullet through the window forced them back, buying more time.

My only regret is that the explosion did not sever the head of the car operator. Even while I was recovering, he was busy building another car. Six more clowns will be hired; six more clowns will filter in and out of the tiny car. In time, they will suffer the same ill-fated mind fuck, eventually turning their fears and torment upon one another. They will have unrelenting thoughts of death toward one another, just like us. Their fates will end, just like ours did.

Through the sugar-filled air of the circus, there are those who will look upon the small car with astonishment as they applaud the exiting clowns. I look upon the car as a mindshattering test of mental will for those who find themselves unfortunate to be inside.

With no more whiskey available, I hold the gun to my temple. My powdered skin welcomes the cold steel as the cops continue their bargaining efforts. Throughout my journey within the car, I was always the last clown out ... and this would be no exception.

K. Trap Jones is an author of horror novels and short stories. With inspiration from Dante Alighieri and Edgar Allan Poe, he has a temptation toward narrative folklore, classic literary works and obscure segments within society. His short stories have appeared in various anthologies and magazines. His novel, *The Sinner* won the 2010 Royal Palm Literary Award. Some of his other novels include *The Charm Hunter, The King's Ox, The Harvester* and more. He can be found lurking around Tampa, FL.

Pint Bottle Press
99¢
DOUBLE-BARREL HORROR
GILDED LILY
the little girl
VIC KERRY

Gilded Lily

by Vic Kerry

Liz stared at the dark pink cross on the plastic dipstick. Her mouth hung loose. She could feel it, but didn't have enough wherewithal to close it. The color on the indicator was too strong to be a false positive. She was pregnant.

Tears formed in her eyes. There had been at least two scares in the past, but this was real. She'd been frightened the other times, but now Liz felt happiness. Her tears were those of joy.

What would James say? They had only been seeing each other a few months. The tears trickling down her cheeks turned cold with fear. She sucked in a great sob. It echoed across the white tile of the bathroom floor.

"Are you okay in there?" James' voice came from the other side of the door.

Liz wiped one eye clear of tears so that she could look to confirm the door was locked. James jiggled it. Then he tapped.

"Nothing," she answered back. "I'm fine."

"Sounds like you're crying."

She sucked down any remaining sobs and wiped her eyes with the heel of her hand. The lock popped out as she turned the door handle, still sitting on the closed toilet lid. The door swung open. James stood framed in the doorway still wearing his sleep clothes. His grey tank top clung to his muscular chest and abdomen. His well-formed shoulders and arms were naked. A pair of blue gym shorts hung over his well-defined legs, and the outline of his business shown through the shiny fabric. He never wore underwear to bed or to work out. If Liz hadn't known better, she might have thought he'd just come back from the gym or a jog.

"I'm pregnant." The words fell out of her mouth like a twenty-pound barbell hitting the floor.

James' mouth sagged into a frown like the muscles had been overworked. Then the edges of his lips curled up, just a little.

"Pregnant?"

Liz nodded.

"Wowwy!"

James sounded like a little boy who'd just gotten a new Huffy. He even danced around in a circle just inside the door. Before she knew it, he'd pulled her up and was hugging her. Tears rolled down his cheeks. She knew that his tears were of joy, too. No grown man yelled *wowwy* unless he was so overjoyed words had left him. He pulled away from her and kissed her on the lips, hard. It wasn't a kiss like she'd gotten on other occasions when someone was happy. It was a kiss of passion.

"You heard me right?"

"Of course I did. I'm going to be a daddy. A *daddy*." James did another twirly-dance move and kissed her again as hard as the first time.

"I thought you'd be mad."

James gave her a look like he never had before. The electrical engineer who could answer any question on *Jeopardy!* looked bumfuzzled. "Why would I be mad?"

"For one thing, we've only been dating a few months."

"And?"

"You've often talked about how getting married was the stupidest thing any two people could do," Liz said.

"It is, but I've also told you how I've always wanted to be a daddy."

"But, what about?"

He kissed her again and pulled her out of the bathroom. They kept kissing as they moved down the hall and back into the bedroom. James lowered her down on the bed. She watched as he stripped off and stood before her. All the sinewy muscles in him seemed taut like a cable ready to burst.

She noticed that it was every muscle.

He crawled onto the bed and started removing her tshirt. They kissed as the cool air washed over her naked breasts. Before she knew it, she laid beside him completely nude, kissing and receiving kisses.

"Don't you think we should talk about some stuff?" she asked between passionate breaths.

"Later."

They made the best love they had ever made. Every inch of her body screamed out in orgasm more times than she had ever experienced with any man. He too seemed to delight in the pleasure more than any other time they had been together.

Afterward, they dozed back off.

***

Liz lies on a bed of pine needles in the middle of a sundappled forest. The aroma of the wild fills her nose with its deep musk. Birds chatter high in the treetops, lost among the mosaic of green foliage. The world is alive around her.

The sun warms her skin and makes her sleepy. Everything is like a fairytale cartoon. She expects to see little gnomes marching by. She can almost hear their happy work song. Liz yawns, bringing in all the tastes of the pine forest like sipping on strong gin. It intoxicates her. Sleep comes with the fuzzy stupor of being drunk. She falls away.

At the edges of sleep, she hears rustling around her. It is not the playful hopping and tussling of sparrows or squirrels. Something sinister moves among the fallen leaves. She tries to rouse herself, but everything moves as if weighed down with years of forest sediment. The noise grows louder, less like rustling and more like feet dragging through the litter.

Liz jerks up with all the force she can muster. As she does, briar vines, sharper than serpents' teeth, shoot up through the pine straw. They twist around her wrists and ankles. A thicker braided rope of the stuff encircles her neck and pulls her back to the ground. The rustling becomes a charge now. Heavy feet tromp through the forest, getting ever near. She looks back as far as she can, but sees nothing but the bright sunlight shining down on her.

More briars sprout from the ground. They wrap around her legs and pull at them. Each little thorn digs into her smooth flesh as the vines wrench her legs open. Now for the first time, Liz realizes that she is naked. Her body tenses and becomes cold as the sun disappears behind a looming shadow.

The air becomes perfumed with the sickly sweet smell of gardenia, and Liz is blinded as more and more vines push up through the ground and wrap over her eyes, mouth and neck. She breathes through her nose, trying to yell for help, but the muzzle of thorns does not allow a syllable out. Panic overtakes Liz as she lies tethered to the ground by a host of living, sawing briars.

As she writhes, a hard, sharp object penetrates her like an evil phallus. It moves in and out. Liz screams into the briar muzzle, but only slices her lips on the sharp edges. Blood enters her mouth as another warm and uncomfortable liquid enters her lower area. She feels it wriggle inside her like worms crawling toward guts.

***

Liz shot up from the prone position, knocking James' arm off her shoulder in the process. A long scream spewed from her throat like a stream of hot vomit. She even tasted the metallic flavor of stomach acid at the back of her mouth.

Everything looked as it should. Her bedroom was halflit by the late morning sun. Black and white pictures of London on the butter-yellow walls. Her reflection stared at her from the dresser mirror across the room. Her hair hung over her face, wet with nightmare sweat. Her bare breasts stood pert and flushed from fear.

James' reflection joined hers. She saw his hand touch her shoulder before she felt it. Anticipating the sharp cuts of the briars from her dream, his callused hand seemed almost velvety soft.

"What's the matter, Sweetheart?" His voice still had remnants of sleep in it.

"Nightmare." Liz kept a tight unblinking stare locked on her reflection.

"Want to talk about it?"

"Not right now."

James climbed out of bed. He walked between Liz and the mirror. Her attention turned to watching his confident strut.

"I'm going to make something for us to eat," he said.

She shook her head. "Don't worry about me. I'm not hungry."

"Nonsense, you've got to eat. There's someone else depending on you now."

James left her alone with her reflection. She covered herself with the sheet. The dream still lingered in her mind. It made her feel dirty. She got to her feet, pulling the sheet along with her and walked into the bathroom to shower.

***

James waited at the bar in the kitchen. He rolled a longneck between his hands. The condensation from the bottle dripped off his little finger. Liz was late. Her appointment for the ultrasound had been at two-thirty. He'd wanted to go so badly, to get the first glimpse of his kid. No child of his would ever have to say he or she didn't have a daddy. James wanted to be there from the start. This ultrasound was the start, but his boss wouldn't let him go. The client they had today was too big.

He'd fidgeted all day long. There was no telling how many times he checked and rechecked the circuits on the prototype before the presentation. He stumbled through most of the discussion of the product with his mind too focused on Liz and the baby. Finally, after the presentation but before the celebratory drinks, the boss sent him home.

The Budweiser should've calmed him down, but it seemed to jazz him up more. A good workout would do the trick, but he didn't want to miss Liz the moment she walked in the door. She'd promised to have the sonar pictures ready. The truth was, and James couldn't deny it, that he was worried. Liz hadn't been eating well. She shied completely away from meat and only had a taste for beets and halfcooked potatoes.

Just strange cravings, she'd said when he expressed his concern. He didn't think it was just that, but let it go to keep down argument.

The front door creaked opened. James slugged a quick swallow of beer and left the kitchen.

"Are you here?" Liz asked, coming down the hall.

James met her before she was halfway there. "Yeah, I'm here." A quick kiss on the lips. "What did the doctor say?"

Before she could answer, he'd taken her hand and pulled her down the hall and into the kitchen. He left her standing by the table as he retrieved his beer and got a bottle of orange juice out of the fridge for her.

"Well, she said that the development is on track."

James sat the juice on the table in front of her. He motioned for her to sit as he did the same.

"What about the potato-and-beets thing?" He slugged another swallow of Bud to keep himself from rattling the words out too quickly.

Liz sat down and let her purse slide off her shoulder to the floor. She opened the orange plastic bottle. "She said it's probably craving, but that I need to be eating a well-balanced diet, and that potatoes and beets exclusively don't qualify." "She said everything's okay, though?" "Yes." Liz smiled and took a drink.

James felt his willpower snap. He'd been trying to keep back his excitement and anxiety, but couldn't anymore. "So where is it?"

"Where's what?" Her voice sparkled with playfulness.

"Don't do that. You know what."

"Oh this." She reached down into her purse and brought out two square photographs.

The black glossy finish caught the light over the table. It looked like she held two squares of shiny onyx. James reached out his hand like a kid grabbing for the last lollipop. She pulled the pictures back. He reached farther over. His fingers almost touched the edge of the paper; she pulled them back again.

"Come on. I almost got fired today because I've been so anxious about this."

Liz smiled and bobbled her head. "Okay."

She handed the pictures over with a fake frustrated huff. James snatched them as if two fifty-dollar bills were attached to them. He stared down at the first one. Nothing seemed clear. A bulbous blob stuck out toward the bottom. A round protrusion was at the top. He shuffled to the next one. It looked the same.

James had seen ultrasounds before. They looked clearer than these. It was almost like Liz's womb was filled with smoke. He frowned. All day on edge for this letdown, he couldn't hide it.

"I know they're a little cloudy." Liz stood beside him.

She touched his hand and spread them so that both pictures showed. Her hand was hot and clammy. She pointed to the round protrusion.

"That's his or her head," she said.

"Where are the eyes and the lips?"

"The doctor said it's all there. She just told me that my amniotic fluid is cloudy."

James outlined the blurry round head with his finger. "Is that normal?"

"She said that she's never seen it personally but heard about it before." Liz put her hand on his shoulder as if to reassure him. She must have sensed his worry. It probably radiated off him like the heat of an incandescent bulb. "Doc said there is nothing to worry about. Just means that we don't get clear Polaroids yet."

James put the pictures down. He grabbed Liz and pulled her into his lap. They kissed, not like two parents-to-be but like lovers.

"Oops." Liz jumped and pulled away a little. "He or she just moved." She flinched again and giggled. "The bugger's going at it."

She took his hand and put it on her stomach. The skin poked out and rolled along as his baby moved. He kept his hand in place and looked at the two blurry photos.

"My baby."

***

The baby turns flips in Liz's stomach. It feels like a bad case of the butterflies. She enjoys every minute of it. No one can imagine the thrill of such a strange feeling, except a mother. Liz likes the idea of being a mother. It took some time to get used to the idea, but she definitely likes it.

She stands cradling her stomach at the edge of a forest. She knows the place. It's where her little baby was conceived. Liz means to tell James that this encounter is the one that blessed them so much, but she always forgets. He would find it funny that their kinkiest encounter produced his baby. Happiness wraps around her like quilts of sunshine. The baby somersaults again. Another tumble plants his or her tiny fetus foot into Liz's bladder.

"Stop that," she says. "I'll have to go pee in the woods."

As if for spite, the baby kicks her bladder again. Now it feels like he or she is pressing down on it, trying to squeeze out the urine. The need to void is too urgent to wait. Liz scuttles into the woods. The trees loom overhead and everything is darker than she would have thought. She stops just inside the gloom and positions herself to void.

Voices come from the edge of the thicket. They near her in a hurry. Not wanting to be caught, Liz pushes deeper into the gloom of the forest. Creatures scurry around just out of vision. The trees creak as they bend in a wind.

She caresses her stomach, cradling it from the fear building inside of her. Liz feels like Red Riding Hood. She's afraid that the wolf might want to steal her basket, her baby. Just as she thinks about running, the urgency to go passes. The baby has moved his or her foot and starts tumbling around again. Then Liz notices a sweet flower smell. It is like nothing she remembers.

There are hints of rose, lavender and gardenia in the scent. She thinks she even identifies magnolia blossom.

"What flower could grow in this gloom?" she asks the baby.

The baby bumps hard into her ribs on the left side. Liz bends to favor the smart. There, just a few steps in front of her, is a lovely growth of flowers. The trumpet blooms are white with purple veining. She's never seen a blossom like it. But she has.

The day that she and James made their precious baby, he'd used one of those flowers on her naked body like a feather. He'd rubbed her everywhere with it, even her lotus. She blushes remembering the passion of that act of lovemaking. Was it that passion that ensured her becoming pregnant?

Lost in memory, Liz doesn't notice how her baby dances inside her. She does not become aware until something sharp scrapes her leg. Whatever it is keeps climbing higher and higher. Liz looks down as a vine, baring one of those strange trumpet blossoms, twines its way toward her belly.

"No!"

She swats at the vine, but it pierces into her navel. Blinding pains radiate from her womb as the flower inches inside her. The baby keeps dancing.

Liz pulls at the vine. The tiny thorns on the stem shred her palms. Then the baby stops moving. She knows that the flower has it. A strong tug begins to pull the vine backward. Her hands still wrapped around the thorns become bloodier.

Then the pain hits like a bullet in her gut. Before she can cradle her stomach, the white and purple bloom bursts from her navel. It is engorged to the size of her fetus. Now the everpresent smell of the flower mixes with that of her blood.

"Thank you," she hears the plant say before she withers to the ground.

***

James stroked Liz's sweat-dampened hair. She'd been having nightmares almost every night. He didn't know what they were about because she would never tell. Tonight, he'd find out.

"So what was it about?"

Liz shook her head. "I don't want to talk about it."

"Was it the same as others you've had?"

"I said I don't want to talk about it." She turned away from him.

"It's just I'm afraid something's wrong. I've been reading lots of magazines about pregnancy, and some say that it can cause psychosis."

Liz looked over her shoulder at him. He saw the devil in her eyes. "So I'm crazy. Is that it?"

"I'm not saying that. I'm just afraid that your hormones and all have you a bit dotty. I guess that would be the word."

"Fine." She rolled to her back with a huff. Her belly stuck up high like an over-ripe melon. "I dreamed that something ripped the baby out of me."

James smiled and felt relief. "That's it."

"What do you mean *that's it*?" She apparently didn't like the relief in his voice.

"Don't get all up in arms at me. Those magazines said that women often dream of something happening to the baby
while they're pregnant. It's normal."

James tried to pet her head like he had before bringing up the subject. She jerked away.

"Do those women have nightmares every night? Do they dream about weird plants going into their bellies and killing the babies?"

"I don't know. Why don't you let me get you some warm milk or hot chocolate to calm you down. I can tell you're shaken up."

Liz's face looked like a *Twilight Zone* version of herself. Everything was shadowed and dark. Her beauty hid behind this grotesque mask of worry and anger. James needed to back off. He knew that. Not too much longer and it would all be over.

"I'm just going to sleep," she said. "We've got an appointment with the ob-gyn soon. We'll bring it up with her."

He weighed his words. They seemed to be heavier than any barbell he'd ever lifted. "Sounds great to me. Goodnight, sweetheart."

She huffed back at him.

"Good night, Baby," he said in his high-pitched baby talk.

A small lump poked out from the side of Liz's belly and moved in a circle. She grunted. James smiled as he switched off the lamp.

***

The nurse pulled Liz's top up over her belly and her pants down off her hips. The exam room—walls were decorated with happy bright pictures of babies with large red flowers. Some of them had loose neckties around their necks and over-sized fedoras.

"These kids are too cute," James said.

The closer the due-date drew, the more saccharine he grew. Liz could hardly stand him some days. Today wasn't one of those. He was too cute himself. She took his hand and squeezed it.

"This is going to be a little bit cold." The nurse squeezed some jelly on her belly.

Goosebumps rose on her skin. A little gasp even escaped her lips. The nurse smiled as if to say she was sorry. The next thing that Liz noticed was the pressure of the ultrasound wand on her flesh. She turned her attention to the monitor at her side.

"Is that the baby?" James asked.

The nurse nodded. James squeezed Liz's hand. She was certain it was to keep from babbling like an idiot; he was too excited.

"It looks clearer than last time," Liz said. "I can see a lot more."

The door opened and the doctor came in. She wore a powder pink lab coat over scrubs.

"It does look a lot clearer," she said. "I'm glad to see that. I thought the fluid would clarify some." She looked at James.

"I'm Dr. Stevenson. You must be daddy."

"Yeah."

Liz could tell by the tone of his voice that James was smiling.

"So let's see if we can find out what this little bundle of joy is." Dr. Stevenson took over from the nurse.

The doctor used more pressure as she moved the wand around on Liz's stomach. It felt less like tickling and more like poking. The baby didn't like it much either. Tiny fists began slamming into her rib cage.

"Look at that," James said. "It's doing Tae Bo."

"I don't have to look. I can feel it."

"He's really giving it to you. I don't think I can remember a little boy so sensitive to the ultrasound," Stevenson said.

"Little boy?" James said.

Liz felt excitement even with the pummeling her insides were taking. She looked over at the ultrasound monitor.

"I'd say so." The doctor pointed to an appendage the size of a pinky finger.

"That's his dingaling?" Liz asked. She didn't even try to keep the wonder out of her voice.

"No, that's got to be his umbilical cord," James said. "There's no way."

"I don't remember ever seeing one that big on an ultrasound, but that's a penis," Dr. Stevenson said.

Liz noticed that hair-like strands floated around the baby. He also hadn't turned so that they could see his face.

"Why hasn't he turned so that we can see his face?" Liz asked.

Dr. Stevenson tried to move the ultrasound wand around to get a view at the baby's face. He seemed to turn away from it, always showing them the back of his head.

"I think he's mad," James laughed. "You've been poking that thing at him too much."

"What are those little strands in there?" Liz asked as a tangled-looking mass of the hairy strands floated by.

"It must be remnants from the cloudiness you've had on the other sonars," Dr. Stevenson said.

The doctor removed the wand. The nurse took a handful of tissue and wiped Liz's belly free of the jelly. It tickled again. The baby started rolling around, but at least he wasn't punching her anymore.

"I think everything's on schedule. You don't have much longer, Liz," Dr. Stevenson said. "You better start coming up with a name for him."

"I'm thinking Louie," James said.

Liz sat up, pulling her shirt down. "Why that?"

"As in Louisville Slugger. Did you see that thing?"

Liz shook her head at the doctor.

"Men," Liz, Dr. Stevenson, and the nurse said together.

***

The day ended up being perfect. The sun was out in the bluebird sky. The temperature was perfect; not too hot, not too cool. Liz and James decided to go on a picnic back to where they had made little Jesse. They had decided on the name just a few hours after the sonogram.

They sat on a quilt at the edge of the woods. James had made sure it was the exact same quilt they had made love on that day nearly nine months before. The major differences were that she felt as big as a whale, and no wine was involved.

"I've dreamed about this place," Liz said after they had eaten lunch. "During some of my nightmares."

"That's odd. I'd figure you'd have good feelings about this place."

Liz looked into the woods. They weren't nearly as dark as in her dreams. Sunlight filtered in everywhere. It looked more like some enchanted forest from a Disney movie than the evil woods of Grimm's fairytale.

"It's not like anything from my dreams. Everything is so bright and cheerful."

"You almost expect to see some mythical creature come walking out; don't you?"

Liz smiled. "I was thinking that myself."

A swift kick met with her ribs. Another jabbed at her spleen or at least where Liz thought her spleen would be. She made a pained expression.

"What's the matter?" James asked.

"The baby has decided to play kung fu again."

A punch landed on a kidney. Another kick slammed into her bladder. Liz floundered around trying to get her footing to stand. James was already on his feet by the time she came close to standing. He helped her up. Once standing, the attacks from inside her slowed down.

"I think that's what he wanted," she said. "Maybe we should walk around. He might go to sleep."

"Does he sleep?"

"I don't care. I just don't want another fit of kicking."

Liz padded off toward the edge of the woods. James followed behind her. The air as they fell into the soft shadows of the trees smelled heavily of pine straw. The whole of the area seemed alive with bustling animals. Birds fluttered overhead. Small creatures rustled in the fallen leaves and pine needles just out of sight.

They followed a path through the trees. No one had cleaned out the path with a machete or ax. It was one of those trails that formed after enough people walked many times over the same place.

"It's nice in here," James said.

He walked behind her because the path wasn't wide enough for them to walk side by side. Liz wished it had been; she would have enjoyed walking hand in hand with him.

"Do you remember the day we made little Jesse?" she asked.

"Yeah."

"You went for a walk in here and came back with that funky purple and white flower. Then you used it like a feather."

"No, I didn't. This is first time I've ever been in these woods." James' voice sounded genuinely confused. "We made little Jesse down by the creek. You know where it comes out of the trees. There were bushes for us to hide behind."

"Quit fooling around. You know that we did it in the wide open on the quilt. You used that blossom all over my body, and I mean *all* over my body."

Liz felt a little aroused just thinking about that kinky day. The baby seemed to be feeling something, too. He pushed against the front of her belly. The pressure grew stronger. Liz felt her skin stretch out, as though small tears radiated from the pressure point. She stumbled forward and off the trail.

"Are you okay?"

James came to her side. The pain increased in her stomach as the baby seemed to push harder and harder against her navel. All Liz could do was shake her head. She rubbed over her belly.

"What is it? Are you having contractions?"

Liz shook her head again. Sharp stinging streaked from her navel toward her spine. She lifted her shirt over her belly. A spider-web of green lines spread from her navel. The lines pulsated. She could feel them beneath her skin.

"What is that?" James reached out to touch the filaments.

"No." Liz knocked his hand away.

She stumbled deeper into the woods, stopping when she hit a tree. The things running across her belly moved as a sharp pain tore through her bellybutton. She looked down to see a long hair-like projection sticking out of her navel. She screamed.

Something larger tore at her belly now. Her internal tendons snapped, and her tissues began ripping from the inside out. The tight skin over her belly burst open as a green mass unfolded itself from her. She crumpled to the leavestrewn ground as the skin on her back flayed open as well.

"My God!" James yelled.

The blood rushing through her ears made it sound as if he had whispered. Her vision turned red, but his face looked frozen in a gaze of utter horror. She tried to speak but couldn't.

"What's happening?" he yelled again. "What are you doing? Stop it before you kill the baby—before this kills *you!*"

A hard convulsion shook through her body. The thing coming out of her drew from her vital fluids. The blood rushed away from head and heart, the sound like water going down a drain. Her skin withered around her as the exquisite pain of the birth faded into an opium-like stupor. Her mind numbed as the baby suckled from her.

James watched as Liz exploded. Something large and green unfolded itself from her stomach as hundreds of threadlike projections shot from her back. She remained alive during this. He saw the horror locked onto her face.

Rage filled James. Whatever had happened to Liz had killed his baby, his boy. He found a heavy limb on the ground beside him. Taking it like a bat, he advanced on the creature. As he drew closer, ready to bash it into nothingness, white trumpet-shaped flowers with variegated purple lines bloomed from the husk of his fiancée. Her body withered as the plant grew larger. The cheeks that had been pudgy with pregnancy collapsed inward until the skin clung to the teeth. Her eyes shriveled to white raisin-like things. Her breasts, once so full with the anticipation of nursing, lay flaccid and drained of anything that had propped them up. Through the hole torn by the plant, James saw her heart beat. It slowed until the movement was barely noticeable.

A sweet smell like the mixture of roses, lavender and gardenia surrounded him. Déjà vu came over him. He'd smelled that scent before not that long ago, but that curious feeling wasn't strong enough to quiet his rage.

James raised the limb over his head. He brought it down, but stopped just short of contact with the thing.

"Daddy." The voice came from the flowers. But not across the air. It appeared in his head. "Daddy, I love you."

He remembered everything now. The day he and Liz had made love on the picnic he had used a flower on her. He'd found it when he'd gone to take a leak. The smell so mesmerized him that he had to show it to her. Something compelled him to rub the bloom all over her body.

"Daddy, I'm lonely."

James dropped his weapon and plucked a blossom from the vine. His boy was going to need a brother.

The Little Girl

by Vic Kerry

Wilberforce kept whining. It was loud and high pitched. Henry couldn't focus with his dog doing that. He looked out of the window to see if he could see anything that might cause the dog to whine. Usually Wilberforce only did that when a storm blew up. Stars spangled the velvety black night. He watched a long time. Nothing changed, but the dog kept whining. Henry couldn't get anything done with him going on like that.

Henry opened the door and stepped onto the stoop. The dog cowered against the far wall. It looked back toward the driveway and whined in terror.

"What is it?" Henry asked as if his dog could answer.

The little red mutt looked at him and then back down the driveway. Henry walked down the steps. He looked toward his driveway. His faithful dog followed him, staying between his legs. Henry's car sat in front of the garage door, and the porch light cast just enough glare to illuminate the back of it. Henry wondered if someone had broken into his garage. If so, they wouldn't find much except boxes from his office that he hadn't had the mental strength or desire to go through. A brand new crib sat under a sheet of plastic, too. It was unused and would stay that way.

Henry took two steps toward his car. The neighbor's dogs started barking at his house. They were coming quickly across the yard. It wouldn't be any time until Wilberforce perked up and took off to chase them away. That didn't happen. Instead the neighbor dogs stopped well short of the light, began whining, and retreated on their own.

Trepidation tumbled in Henry's gut. Something had spooked the dogs. He knew that a stranger never made any of them kowtow. They would usually charge full bark and bare teeth. Henry started to take another step when he saw movement on the other side of his car. The shadows were too deep for him to get a good look.

"Who's there?" he asked.

He blinked, and when he opened his eyes, two red orbs looked at him from the shadows behind his car. They stared at him a little over waist high. Henry's breath caught in his throat.

A little girl stepped into the light. Her brown hair touched her shoulders. Her eyes were blue. She wore a light blue dress like *Alice in Wonderland*. He felt a little silly for being so scared. He'd been scaring himself a lot, lately.

"Are you lost?" he asked.

She shook her head. His dog whined louder and pressed harder into his legs.

"Don't be scared," he said to the girl. "Where are you supposed to be?"

"Right here."

The little girl smiled. It almost spread from ear to ear. Henry took a step back when he saw her teeth. They looked like those of a mako shark. Each was sharp, jagged, and set at weird angles.

"I think you're mistaken," he said, trying to sound calm and hoping a little that he was hallucinating.

"No mistake, Henry Davidson. This is where I'm supposed to be."

His blood ran cold. Her eyes glimmered red. Henry almost tripped over his dog as he bounded back up the steps onto the stoop and into his house. A locked door might not do anything to stop that thing, but it made Henry feel safer. Wilberforce whined, then barked. Henry felt a pang of regret for leaving his pet out there with the thing. There was nothing he could do now. The dog could run; surely she wouldn't be able to catch him. Wilberforce was fast enough to catch rabbits.

Despite his terror, Henry stood by the window but dare not look out. A thousand thoughts crossed his mind as he waited, listening for what that little girl-thing would do next. His dog whined. It wasn't running away. Perhaps it was so struck with terror that it couldn't.

He remembered freshman year in college, when he'd met Jeana, his wife, in a project group. His psychology 101 professor lectured at length about unethical studies. As poor Wilberforce whined outside with the child monster, Henry remembered the study about the dogs who were trapped on the electrified grates. They were so afraid by the torture that at a certain point they just gave up. The professor called it learned helplessness. Henry hoped like everything that hadn't happened to *his* dog.

"Come here, puppy," the girl said. Her voice sounded clear like no pane of glass separated Henry from her. "I won't hurt you."

Wilberforce whined and yelped. Henry looked out the window through separated louvers of the blinds. The demon Alice bent over and petted his dog. Wilberforce wagged his tail. He looked pleased. Henry thought perhaps he'd been hallucinating after all. He hadn't been in his right mind moments before all this happened. Everything could just be a bad trip. The little girl was probably lost. She might even be mentally challenged. His mind was soft, spongy, addled by the pills. An empty bottle of Xanax sat on the end table. Jeana had taken them after the miscarriage. After she left him that morning, the pills had remained behind. He'd polished them off with three gulps from a nice, cold Budweiser.

"Are you all right?" he whispered, looking out the window at the girl and dog.

She turned to him. Her shark teeth bared in a grin. "We're fine."

Now Wilberforce looked up at him. The dog's eyes glowed. He appeared to be smiling, too. His lips pulled back to reveal rows of mako teeth. Henry stifled a scream, dropped the louver, and stumbled backward. She had turned his dog into whatever she was.

Drowsiness dragged on his attention and dulled his acuity of thought. Fuzzy clouds winged across his vision. The Xanax kicked into full effect. Maybe all that would make the horrible child go away.

"Mary, Mary quite contrary, how does your garden grow?" the girl's voice sing-songed the nursery rhyme.

Henry blinked hard to make sure he had actually come into the house. He stood in his living room, alone except for his empty bottle of Xanax and a full .38 special.

"With despair, fear, and Xanax that works too slowly," the girl continued.

"Who are you?" he whispered.

"You know who I am."

Henry did know her. He'd known her from the very moment he'd seen that evil gapped-tooth smile. The thing that bothered him was why. The girl-thing had no reason to be there. What had he done to deserve the torture?

"You know why I'm here."

She heard his thoughts even when they weren't directed at her. He heard her voice in his head. They were attached psychically. Of course they were. Since she had been conceived, they had been attached by a telepathic umbilical cord. The shark-toothed girl was his daughter, Sophia. He'd heard her voice for nearly nine months through their special link. Her angelic face still haunted his dreams since the time of Jeanna's miscarriage. He knew the pain she'd felt *in utero* those desperate minutes during the spontaneous abortion. All his hopes and dreams disintegrated the moment of her death. Everything had left him—hope, wants, and the desire to live. All that had brought him to this moment: a gut full of pills and a loaded pistol.

Henry opened the blinds. Sophia still played with Wilberforce. The dog no longer appeared frightened. He rubbed his head against the girl and even rolled onto his back so that she could scratch his belly.

"What do you want?" Henry asked.

Sophia looked up at him. She smiled. "You know."

"No, I don't."

He had no idea why his daughter had come to him. The last time he saw her she was an incomplete baby. Her eyes were still closed. Never was she six or seven. Not even in their telepathic communication was she that old.

His head felt swimmy again. He sat on the sofa but twisted the blinds open so he could keep an eye on Sophia. Colors started to dance around in his vision. They swirled in tiny dots, pulsating with Technicolor rhythm. The part of his vision beyond the swirl began to streak like water washing down a pane of glass, until all the background faded to black. Henry sat, staring at the dazzling light show. His consciousness became soft. The swirling became faces floating in space. They contracted into hideous uncanny visages. His life became a kaleidoscope of kabuki masks. All this changed into a line floating in the dark void. It moved in small twitches, matching the cadence of the ambient sound in Henry's head. It thrummed to the rhythm of a heartbeat.

The line formed a mouth with a row of shark's teeth. The teeth moved as the mouth opened and closed.

"Jesus love me. This I know, for the voices tell me so. Dead babies to him belong. You thought in Heaven, but you were *wrong*," Sophia's voice sang with the enthusiasm of a Sunday school class.

Henry opened his eyes. The harshness of the light sent a spike of pain through his temple. It took a moment for the brilliant flare of red that almost obscured his vision to clear. Once things fell into focus, he saw Sophia standing in front of him. She smiled with all her shark teeth bared. His precious baby had come to take him.

"Why you?" he asked.

"Because I'm the reason for all of this," she said. "You felt me from the start. We talked. We laughed, and then you killed me. It's only fair that I should usher you over."

"I killed you?" he asked. "I loved you."

"Don't you remember?"

At that moment, he did. Jeana had become very distant during the last few weeks before the miscarriage. She said she wasn't sure if she loved him anymore. Every reason she gave revolved around Sophia. Henry had never loved anything more than his wife. It turned out that even with his daughter, with Sophia on the way, he still could love no one more than his wife. The thought of losing her made him wish they'd never gotten pregnant.

With all the thoughts he could muster, he sent an image to his unborn daughter of death and Hell. His thoughts turned the amniotic fluid acidic. Sophia burned in her mother's womb.

"I don't want to die," he said to his monstrous daughter.

"Too late."

***

Wilberforce whined at the door. Henry couldn't get anything accomplished with him carrying on like that. At that moment, it didn't matter. He saw his daughter beckoning to him like an angel at the end of a faraway white light. Only when he got to her and held her hand did she open her mako shark teeth.

About the Author

Vic Kerry is the author of the novels, *The Children of Lot*, *Revels Ending*, and the forthcoming, *As an Old Memory*. He lives in Alabama with his wife, five dogs and cat. Keep up with his releases and other random stuff by friending him on Facebook.

Pint Bottle Press
99¢
DOUBLE-BARREL HORROR
JUST ONE POUND
Meetings with the Devil
J.C. MICHAEL

Just One Pound

by J.C. Michael

"I should go back there and give the bastards a piece of my mind. Don't you think?"

"Nobody'd blame you."

"I mean, it's scandalous, bullying someone when they can't defend 'emselves. They oughtta be given a taste of their own medicine, made to suffer."

"Yeah, damn right."

"Are you even listening to me?"

"Course I am. Sorry. Just got shit of my own t' think about, y' know? Jo's in one of her moods again. Christ mate, I give her everything."

"Too right y' do. Including the odd black eye and a nasty itch once in a while."

"Fuck you, Tone. We can't all be Mr. Perfect Fucking Husband."

"Sorry. That w' below th' belt. I'm hardly in our lass' best books m'self, not with all this crap going on. And now she's blaming me. I've had enough of it to be fair."

"Can't blame you, mate. You've had a couple of rough years. You ready for another?"

"Yeah, go on, and get me a short while you're at it."

"You're a cheeky twat, Tone. How come I always end up out of pocket when you're around?"

A fresh round of drinks on the table, a pint of lager apiece with double Grouses for dessert, Gary Mills sat back in his chair, folded his arms over his chest, and took in a deep breath; "Right then, let's put my problems aside 'cos you're spot on, buddy. I've only m'self t' blame while your woes ain't even your own fault."

"Jo'll come 'round. She always does," said Tony Kirk, Gary's long-time drinking partner, and even longer-time best friend. He reached across the table for his pint. "Cheers." As Tony raised the glass to his lips, the soggy beermat stuck to the bottom before falling onto the table. He put his glass down next to it, picked up the soft, square, piece of cardboard, and started pulling it to pieces.

"Maybe not this time, but let's leave it." Gary took a drink of his pint. "You lost the recording then?"

"Well that part's my fault, innit. They took it off me when I stormed into the office. Said it was illegal to make covert films, and that they could have me locked up. Before I knew what was going on it was outta my hand and into a desk drawer." The beermat was in pieces now, pieces Tony poked around the tabletop with the tip of his index finger.

Gary downed his Grouse, winced, and with a strong blow sent the beermat pieces scattering. "You want to bust in and get it back?"

Tony swept the table clean and sighed. "Don't be daft. It'll be long gone. It showed everything. The fuckers were nipping her, stealing her snacks, shouting at her. Man, it was disgusting. The old lady's got this teddy, right, only a little thing but it comforts her. This fat bitch kept offering it to her, then pulling it away. Teasing her like. Did it half a dozen times or so until poor Mary was crying her eyes out. Shit, that's the bit what made Beth crack up when I showed her. It was fucking degrading. She said 'Tony Oliver Kirk, you need to be a man and do something about this. I told you it was going on, and all you did was say I was paranoid. Well, now look. You've got your proof so do something about it.'"

"So you went down to the office waving your proof around, and they took it off you?" Tony said nothing.

"No wonder she's pissed."

***

With the two old friends updated on each other's own particular problems, the conversation turned to the usual topic; sport. Football received top billing, but the cricket and boxing provided a strong undercard. By half ten the pair of them had moved on to their usual reminiscing about their youth. It was a regular ritual, involving stories they both knew by heart, but with the rose-tinted memory of the past helping to keep the dreary grey of the present out of their hearts and minds, at least for a short while.

"Mind if I join you?"

Tony and Gary fell silent, both of them looking at the man who had spoken as if he had an additional head perched on his rounded shoulders. People didn't just come up and ask to join you in the pub; it wasn't a bloody wine bar where suitwearing types could "network".

"Do we know you?" asked Gary as he squinted for a closer look.

"No, but I can soon rectify that. I'm Albert." The man offered a fat hand gleaming with sweat.

Gary ignored the gesture. "Got a surname to go with that?"

"Of course. Now may I sit with you gentleman? I'm quite happy to recharge your glasses in exchange for a few moments of your time."

Tony looked at Gary, Gary looked at Tony. They nodded at each other, and gestured for Albert to take a seat.

"You mentioned a drink?" Gary said.

"Yes, I did, but business first."

Gary made to speak, but the words never left his mouth as Albert raised a finger to his lips and gently said "shush."

Tony was astounded. He'd never seen his friend quietened like that in the twenty-odd years of knowing him.

"Enough prattling, Gareth, you'll get your drink all in good time. Now Anthony."

"It's Tony. Only my grandmother calls me Anthony."

"Yes," Albert said, "now Anthony, I couldn't help but overhear that you have a little problem. Some people have slighted you, yes? Hurt you and your family in unspeakable ways? And to make matters worse the situation has been exacerbated by your own personal failings in the eyes of your wife? Am I right? Of course I am. What a sorry predicament to find oneself in."

"Like I said, it's Tony, and I'm not over keen on you eavesdropping on our conversation, to be honest."

"Me neither," Gary said, "and it doesn't help that I only follow half the crap that's coming out of your mouth. I think you'd better jog on, fella, before you get a boot up your arse."

For a barely perceptible moment a sneer of contempt danced across Albert's face, but then it was gone, a warm smile replacing it. Albert took Gary's gaze and held it as he slid a twenty-pound note across the sticky table. "Go and get the drinks, Gareth, and take your time."

Gary took the twenty, stood, and turned toward the bar. "I'll think I'll have a slash and nip out for a fag while I'm up. Might pop a couple of quid in the bandit, too."

Tony was dumbstruck. His friend was unsteady on his feet and stumbled as he walked toward the toilets, but the further he got from the table, the more control he gained over his gait.

"I hope he has some change for the gambling machine. I could have given him an additional pound or two. The odd pound here and there is nothing really, is it?" Albert chuckled to himself, leaving Tony to wonder what had been so funny. He drew a blank.

"Anthony. I know someone who can help." The humor was gone; Albert looked as serious as an undertaker. "We can help."

Tony didn't reply. There was something off about the sweaty, podgy man beside him. Even if he, or the *someone* he referred to, could help, he wasn't sure if he would want it. A nagging feeling at the back of his subconscious appeared to know that the path opening up to him was not an advisable course to take.

"That's right, Anthony. You need to think carefully about what we are proposing. But we can help you. Help Beth. Help Mary. We. Can. Help."

As Albert looked at him the uncomfortable feeling began to lift. The man's face was a round moon slick with perspiration but his eyes were piercing. Tony's thoughts shifted, he could see that Albert was right; God knew he needed help, and here he was being offered it out of the blue. He'd thought about going to the Police about Mary but he'd had run-ins with the law for most of his adult life. Only petty stuff but still, going to them for assistance didn't sit easy with him. For a start they'd find it hard to believe a word he said, considering he'd spun more tales than J.K.

Rowling over the years. Surely there couldn't be any harm in listening to whatever the wannabe Samaritan was offering. As Albert looked deeper into his eyes Tony began to relax even further; "You can help?"

"Yes. We certainly can. We can deal with your problem in a manner befitting the crime. My associate has a set of skills that allow him to deal with those types of people. Why not come and meet with him. You may as well." "I may as well," Tony said.

By the time Gary got back to the table, Albert and Tony were gone.

***

Tony didn't know if it was fog, mist or pollution that smothered the streets as he and Albert walked. Whatever it was it swallowed anything above three stories high, and brought a clogging claustrophobia to the outdoors that weighed down on him as much as his problems. Albert strode along a few paces ahead, his breath blowing smoke in the air like a sleeping dragon.

"So how exactly do you help people? I don't want to get dragged into anything too shady."

Albert slowed a little. "You'll get an explanation once we reach our destination. Suffice to say we give people what they deserve, plus a little interest to get the message across."

"Are you guys vigilantes? You know, like *Death Wish* or *Taken* or something?"

"Enough of the questions, and I am more than aware of what a vigilante is without the need of references from popular culture." He started walking again as soon as Tony caught up with him. His pace, and breathing, were quicker now, the puff of his breath more steam train than slumbering beast.

"You know Cliff Silk, don't you?" Albert said as they turned a corner.

They hadn't walked far, but Tony didn't recognize the street they had entered, despite him having lived his whole life in the area. He thought it must have been the combination of damp, suffocating fog and the alcohol that was throwing off his bearings, but there was also something otherworldly of the night. He shivered. "He worked at the car parts factory same as me. Different line, different shifts, but yeah, I knew of him. Lost an eye in a mugging."

"Ironic though, wasn't it," Albert said, "that he should be blinded by someone looking to steal his phone. After all, his phone had already been stolen, hadn't it? At least he'd reported it so prior to his ex-girlfriend's nude exposure all over Facebook, Twitter and Instagram."

"Did you have something to do with it?" Tony said, stopping.

"Perhaps." Albert came to a stop. "His ex-girlfriend's father didn't believe that his precious daughter's newfound infamy was an accident. Perhaps he thought it was premeditated revenge porn, and that the police should have done something about it. And perhaps, when they didn't, he met a man in a bar who offered to help make amends."

"I'm not sure about this."

"It doesn't matter." Albert knocked on a door to his left. "We're here, and my associate is expecting you."

***

Almost simultaneous with the door opening, Albert moved behind Tony and, with his palm at the small of his back, guided him through it. Tony began to protest but the door shut with a click of finality.

"Come along." Albert guided him left through a second door.

To Tony the room they entered brought to mind an executive's office, even though he'd never set foot in one and only had TV and movies to go by. The wood-paneled walls were covered in expensive-looking paintings. A large desk had two empty chairs in front, and a single larger chair on the far side. Behind that was a wall of thick, old-fashioned looking books. Everything was dark wood and leather, a room which quietly assured expense and quality.

Much as the front door had shut behind him, so did the door to the office, only this time Albert hadn't followed him in. Instead, he heard a different voice.

"Albert tells me you have a problem, the sort of problem nobody can really help you with."

With no introduction, it was straight down to business. The owner of the voice walked around Tony, gesturing for him to sit as he did so. Tall and thin with a ramrod straight back, he made Tony think of a police officer, an image enhanced by his black suit and white shirt. He wore a black and gold tie, and his hair was a silvery grey cut close to the scalp. Never a fan of authority, Tony felt increasingly uncomfortable with the situation, the evening becoming ever more strange and sinister with each passing moment, and he wished he was at home with Beth and their young daughter.

"That's right enough, but I'm not sure you'll be able to help either. It might be best if I save wasting your time and head off home. The offer's appreciated but..."

"I'll be the judge of whether I can help you or not." The man settled into his own seat.

"But."

"Let us dispense with the buts. If I wasn't interested in your case, you wouldn't be here. So settle yourself down into that chair and humor me with a brief synopsis of the matter at hand."

Tony stood there bewildered. The man in the chair sighed. "Do me a favor and pass me an apple and the knife off the dresser over there. Whilst you are up, pour yourself a glass of scotch. Then, sit back down, and tell me what the problem is."

Tony followed the instructions initially, then deviated from them by downing his drink and pouring himself a second before sitting back down.

"It's my mother-in-law. She's been in a home six months now," a pause for a drink, "I know a lot of blokes can't bard their other half's mothers, but Mary was always sound with me, even with my faults. Beth, that's my wife, well she's been saying for months she thought her mam was being abused, that she had bruises and that. Doesn't help that Mary's off in ga-ga land and doesn't know the day of the week half the time. Anyway, I admit it, I didn't believe her. Old folks fall, right?"

"Yes they do." The man slowly peeled the apple. He pointed the knife at Tony, "Continue."

"So, we got one of them HD cameras and hid it on top of the wardrobe. Decent bit of kit actually, and not a bad price.
If you fancy anything like that, I can..."

"The matter in hand, Mr. Kirk."

"Oh, yeah, sure. Next day we went back to see if we'd caught anything, and Beth was right. We only had footage of that one night, but it were enough. The staff, fucking vicious bastards the lot of them." Tony shook his head.

A slice of apple popped into the man's mouth and he chewed slowly, as if in thought. "Why not take your evidence to the authorities?"

Tony took a drink and then spoke to it, rather than the man who had asked the question, "Can't. Lost it."

"How?"

"They took it off me." His voice was that of a child sitting before his headmaster for the first time.

"How unfortunate," said the man with a smile born of amusement, not empathy. "But you could still go and tell the police."

"Me and the police don't exactly get on."

"Why, that shouldn't make a difference."

"Shouldn't and doesn't are two different things. Maybe I should go to the cops, but…"

The man looked at him sternly. "There you go again. But this. But that. But my arse. Why can't you go to them?"

"Because I supplement my income selling on a few nicked bits and pieces and counterfeit fags my cousin ships in from Turkey, okay? The police know it and think I'm scum because of it. Christ, half the money I make I've spent on keeping the old dear in that bloody home, so that a bunch of twats can batter her and take the piss."

"I'm sure the police would help. It isn't like you're gangster number one. If you were, you could deal with your situation properly."

The slight went over Tony's head. "You're probably right. That's what Beth'll want to do. I guess I've wasted your time."

The man stood, the action causing him to loom over Tony in a way enhanced by the wide shadow he threw on the wall behind him. "You haven't. Besides, help you they might, but not like I can. I operate unfettered by the law, unless you wish to take a more Old Testament view of crime and punishment, in which case, I am a perfect fit. I punish in kind, a service that modern law enforcement are unable to provide.

You'd like that wouldn't you?"

"Yes." Tony looked up from his empty glass.

"You want them to pay?"

"Yes."

"To suffer."

"Yes, but..."

"Fuck the buts, man. There are no buts. You want them to suffer, it's only right that they should. We have a deal, don't we? You and I? I'll take care of these people for you, and you can tell your wife that revenge has been served. I'll get my coat."

The man was already at the door, and Tony could feel the situation running away from him. Everything was moving too fast for him to think. He needed time to consider his options, as he'd never been the sharpest knife in the drawer and always needed that shade more time than he ever seemed to be allowed. Tonight was a classic example, with events following a course that appeared largely out of his control.

"Hang on. I said I'd like it, but I haven't agreed to anything. What do you get out of it?"

The man paused, his hand on the ornate door handle, and his knuckles white with the grip he had upon it. "Oh, don't worry about that. There's no financial charge for my services. I shall merely have my pound of flesh when all's said and done, but we can deal with that later. Honestly, I do this for fun, and because the people I deal with deserve it. You never see Batman sending out invoices, do you? So come along, Anthony, let us conclude our negotiations. I've told you my terms. Have we got ourselves a deal?" He held out his other hand as he spoke.

Even afforded the time to think, Tony's mental abilities were restricted by both nature and nurture. Those bastards at the home had messed with his family, and brought no end of grief into his life. They deserved all they got. "Fuck it. Sure we do."

He took the still unnamed man's hand and shook it. The hand was cold, as though there was no life within it, and his smile was unbelievably wide.

****

No sooner had the nameless man departed than Albert entered the room.

"I'm so glad that we'll be doing business together." He took a large painting of the crucifixion down from the wall to reveal a T.V screen behind it.

"I should be going," Tony said. "Beth's had Courtney all night and she'll want a rest before the night feed." The statement was true, but presented as an excuse to leave rather than a genuine concern for his daughter's feeding routine. He wanted to get away as soon as possible, and felt sick to the core. Had he just put out a hit on the care-home staff? He wasn't sure; he'd never put one out before.

"Oh, no," Albert said. "You stay right where you are while I fix you another drink. It's time for the show. Watch Hector work his magic."

The T.V came on and there, on screen, was the sign outside the home—Rainbow Islands. There was no way the man, Hector, could have gotten there so fast. There had barely been enough time for him to leave the house, but there he was, grinning into the camera.

"Is this thing on?" he said. Tony noticed that Albert had his phone to his ear, and on screen Hector plucked his own phone from the breast pocket of his shirt. His jacket and tie were gone, and his sleeves were rolled up. He looked like a man ready to get down to work. Dirty work.

"We can hear you, sir," Albert said.

Tony looked into the fresh drink Albert passed him and placed it on the desk. They must be drugging him. It was the only explanation.

"Considering your previous camera-related activities, I'm sure you will enjoy this, Anthony. I'm going to show you how it's done."

The camera turned away from Hector and settled into the kind of view Tony regarded as First Person Shooter, the image swaying slightly as Hector walked toward the entrance to Rainbow Islands Respite Home. Tony could only assume the camera was hung around Hector's neck as he could see both of Hector's hands, one occupying each of the bottom corners of the screen, the fingers wriggling as though warming up for a piano recital.

As Tony watched, the right hand disappeared from view.

Then the left hand pushed open the front door.

Tony recognized the member of staff sitting behind a reception desk to the left, although the name eluded him.

"I'm here about Mary," Hector said, voice coming from the speaker bar beneath the T.V.

"Is there a problem?" The tone was surly and gruff. "As since it's the middle of the night I guess you don't need me to tell you that visiting..."

The right hand flashed back into view smashing into the staff member's face and knocking him off his chair. The camera lurched violently from side to side as Hector vaulted over the reception desk to land astride the prostrate figure, his knees either side of his head. Vince — that was his name. Tony remembered it now. Vince. He deserved a good kicking, and Tony began to relax.

"Who said anything about visiting?"

The snarl stabbed through the speaker as Tony watched Hector's right hand smash down into Vince's face again. There was something held in the fist. Tony shifted in his seat, as though moving could give him a better angle to view what was secreted in Hector's hand. It was a futile move, and doubly unnecessary as Hector eased his grip to show the gleaming pair of needle-nose pliers to the camera while Vince struggled beneath him. Hector's weight must have exceeded appearances, for he sat firm and, despite Vince bucking beneath him like an unbroken steer, he remained unmoved.

"You're the fucker that likes to nip old ladies, aren't you? I can smell it on you. You're a bully. A pathetic bully!" Hector punched Vince in the face once more, leaving his nose a squashed mess. "Well, I'm the bully now."

Using his left hand Hector pulled Vince's right up to the side of his head, and used his bare forearm to press down on his mouth. This served to stifle the scream that came as he fixed the pliers over one of Vince's fingers and then, with a vicious twist, broke it. Tony tried to look away, but Albert placed a flabby palm on each side of his head and held it straight.

"Don't even think of closing your eyes, Anthony. Hector wouldn't appreciate it. You watch the harvest you've sown and take it all in, for this is justice in action."

"But this is going too far. Call him and tell him to stop."

"Quit whining," Albert said. "I thought you were an angry young man who would enjoy our sport, but you sound like a whinging bitch."

Snap. A second finger was broken. *Snap.* A third. *Snap, snap,* four and the thumb.

Vince was biting into Hector's arm, causing it to bleed all over his face where it mingled with his own blood, but neither man seemed to care. They were locked in an embrace of mutual mutilation which was suddenly reversed by Hector so as to give him access to Vince's left hand.

Snap, a sixth finger. *Snap*, seven, *snap*, eight, *snap* nine.

Tony braced himself for the final snap, his head still held firm by Albert, but it never came. Instead there was a stomach-turning squelch, and a faint pop, as Hector stabbed the pliers down into Vince's left eye. The camera angle then slowly panned out as Hector stood, showing the extent of the damage wrought upon Vince's hands and face. Vince's body twitched and spasmed between Hector's legs. Tony retched. Albert passed him a tissue.

"How'd you like that, Tone, me old matey?" said Hector's voice from the T.V.

"Tell him to stop," Tony said.

"He wouldn't listen even if I did," Albert said. "Once he starts something, he always finishes it."

***

It took five minutes of wandering the corridors of Rainbow Islands before Hector came across another member of the staff. Five minutes in which Tony pleaded to Albert's deaf ears that the madness needed to stop. Five minutes to listen to Hector whistling as though he hadn't a care in the world, hadn't just murdered a man in cold blood, and hadn't blood on his hands and bite marks on both arms.

"So who's that, Anthony?" Albert gestured at the screen. Hector had swung open a door to find a staff member asleep on the bed. The legitimate owner of the bed, a stick-thin old man in striped pajamas that looked like they belonged in a concentration camp, was dumped in the armchair by the window like a forgotten doll in a nursery.

"Mike. He's called Mike. Look, let's forget about this. Call Hector and — Shit." On screen Hector held a knife in his right hand, a sponge in the left. "What's he going to... ?"

Albert had no call to answer, as the answer presented itself on screen. The sponge went over Mike's mouth; the knife plunged into his stomach and sliced across it. Tony gagged as blood poured from the wound, soaking the sheets. Hector discarded the knife and plunged his bloody fist into the gash. He was feeling around for something, his investigations caught on camera, and then Tony watched through slitted eyes as he pulled out a handful of what Tony believed to be intestine onto the bed. Tony vomited watery brown puke down his shirt.

Albert tutted, and offered another tissue. "Such a small capacity for blood is surprising when there is so much death and depravity on screen these days. It amazes me how weak you people really are. Playing your games and watching your movies, you think nothing of the thousands of deaths played out before you in ever more elaborate ways for your gratuitous entertainment, yet as soon as fantasy becomes

reality, you buckle. It's pathetic."

The sounds of squelching from the speakers turned Tony's stomach once more, but he fought back the urge to add to the stinking puddle on the floor. He wouldn't give Albert the satisfaction. "Turn the fucking sound off."

"*Turn the fucking sound off,*" Albert mocked him. "Do that and I'll be the next poor soul to be disemboweled. Wasn't it Mike who stole the snacks you left for your mother-in-law? Doesn't he deserve to have his insides emptied of that which he took ... which was not his to take?"

"This can't be happening," moaned Tony. "What the fuck are you two? Is it a religion thing? Is that it? You can believe what you want, but don't do it in my name. You've got to stop him. Please!"

As Tony pleaded the screen showed Hector's hands as he washed them in the room's small sink. In the mirror above was Hector's face, blood-splattered and beaming. Behind him was the butchered corpse of Mike, with what seemed to be more of him spread about the bed than could possibly be left inside him.

"Enjoying the entertainment?" Hector's voice boomed from the speaker.

"Fuck you!" Tony shouted.

Albert clipped him around the ear.

"I hope you are keeping our guest in line, Albert. I expect he's wavering a little by now. He needs to consider the tragedy of life, and sanctity of death. I think we'll do one more." The screen showed Hector's killing hands as he dried them on a coarse, grey towel. "And then call it a night."

***

"Is that the woman who taunted her?" Albert said. "I believe her name is Molly Ridgeway, age 42, of Snipe Close." He sat behind the desk now, his feet up and a cigarette in hand. He'd offered Tony one, but Tony hadn't answered. Tony was beyond words. The sick was drying to a crust on his trousers, and the smell stung his eyes.

On screen Hector sat opposite a plump woman he'd found in the canteen. In his right hand was a heavy looking pistol, the type that held six bullets in a revolving cylinder. His left hand wasn't in view.

"You think it's nice to tease people with things they care for?" said Hector's disembodied voice. "How would you like it, you callous bitch? We should go for a walk and think about it." The barrel of the gun flicked in a way that said *Get up and move.*

Tony watched as Molly stood. She looked scared out of her wits, and he couldn't help but feel sorry for her. There was no way this was in proportion to what they had done. They deserved to lose their jobs. They should have had to pay compensation. But they shouldn't be getting massacred like teens in a slasher flick. Tony wanted Molly to escape, but he doubted she would. No jury would determine her guilt, nor judge pass sentence. All she faced was a cold-blooded executioner looking for his hat-trick.

The screen showed Molly's back as she walked, following the single, curt instruction of "outside." She almost collapsed when she saw what had befallen her colleague at reception.

Once into the car park Hector barked a further directive to the distraught woman, "The BMW, over there." She reached the car.

"Open the boot."

She opened the boot, and gasped.

Tony watched as Hector reached in and brought out a small dog, a terrier of some kind if he was identifying it rightly. It barked happily to see Molly, who Tony assumed to be its owner. Hector cocked the hammer of the gun and passed it to her.

"Shoot him!" Tony shouted at the screen. "Shoot the lunatic!"

"Come on, Anthony," Albert said. "Do you take him for a fool? It's out of sight, but I'd bet you there's another gun pointing right at her fat gut."

Hector's voice came from the speaker; "Spin the cylinder, point the gun at your dog's head, and pull the trigger."

Sobbing could be heard in the background. The camera pointed at the dog, and Tony was glad he couldn't witness the distress that must have been etched across the poor woman's face.

"You want your dog to live, don't you? I've got a full clip here, no empty chambers. If you don't shoot, and I do, it's bye-bye guaranteed. What is your dog's name, by the way?" The second gun was now in view, shiny, black and modern.

"Answer me, Molly, or the dog whose name I do not know goes to doggy heaven."

"Wilson," Molly croaked through the speaker.

"I can't take this," Tony said.

"For crying out loud, show some compassion! How do you think she's feeling?" Albert said.

"Right, right, Wilson. If I shoot, then it's bye-bye Wilson. If you shoot, it's only a one-in-six chance he dies. Now spin the cylinder, Molly. There's a good sport."

Molly brushed her hand against the gun, but only enough to move it a couple of chambers. She was crying floods of tears now, but Hector's exasperated sigh could still be heard.

"Spin the cylinder, or the devil help me I'll put that gun to the side of your head and pull the trigger until it blows your fucking brains out. And then I'll kill your mutt anyway."

This time the spin was strong, and Tony was amazed as, without pause, she pointed the gun at the dog and pulled the trigger. *Click.*

"Do it again."

She did. *Click.*

"And again."

A third click, and then the gun dropped to the ground with a crash.

"You, my dear," said Hector's voice through the speakers, "are a heartless bitch. Your dog, is one lucky fucker. You, on the other hand, have no luck left."

Tony watched Hector pick up the gun, spin the cylinder, and shift the camera expertly so it captured the moment center-screen as he calmly shot Molly in the face.

***

"The job's done, Anthony," said Hector, "so we had better give due consideration to payment."

"You'd better listen carefully." Albert was back on his feet now.

The camera moved again and appeared to be set down on the roof of the car. Tony could hear barking, then the sound of a gunshot. The barking stopped. Seconds later Hector's smiling face looked into the camera and at Tony. His collar was turned up, and he was knotting his tie. Both collar and tie were stained with blood.

"So, Anthony, if you cast your mind back, you will recall that you were clearly told that a pound of flesh would be required," Hector said in a voice so clear he sounded right back in the room, and not standing in the Rainbow Islands car park with a dead woman at his feet.

"You're insane," Tony said.

Albert leant close. "And you are an idiot talking to a television screen. Then again, I would still keep your mouth shut if I were you. As things stand, the donor of said flesh is yet to be determined. I'd hate for your mother-in-law to be selected after you've been so good as to have her tormentors dealt with. Or your wife, for that matter. Or your friend, Gary, he must be wondering where you've got to. If you yap on too much, Hector will know. Believe me, he'll know, and he might just decide that you're volunteering to provide the payment yourself without negotiation."

"Anthony, you still there?" Hector said from the screen. "Albert, how's he doing? We need to upgrade to something that works both ways for this, you know. I feel like I'm missing out. Yes, a pound of flesh, that's my fee. Human flesh, too. If you would be so kind as to give some thought as to how you propose to settle up, we can have a chat when I return.

It's just a pound, which is what, only four good burger's worth? So don't worry too much about it. Speak soon." And, with that, the screen went blank.

***

The wait seemed like an eternity for Tony as he sat with a now silent Albert. Eventually, he heard the outer door open, then shut. A couple of footsteps later the door to the office opened to reveal a blood-splattered Hector who appeared ten years younger than when they had first met. In his hand was a small black briefcase, with blood dripping out of it.

"Please accept my apologies for taking so long. That fat woman took a while to check over. There were some promising cuts, but nothing that really floated my boat."

"I don't know what you think..." Tony was being talked over even before he'd said that much.

"Perks of the job, Anthony, perks of the job. You know how it is, somebody pays you to dig a hole in the ground, and you come across something valuable in the process. A ring perhaps, or a coin. You would take it, would you not?"

Tony said nothing, his mind collapsing beneath the weight of the situation.

"Albert, can you get me a book, please?"

Albert did as he was asked, and removed one of the books from the shelves before laying it on the desk.

"I'm a collector, you see." Hector flicked through the unusually thick pages of the book. Each page had a picture on it. Pictures of a type Tony recognized—tattoos. His stomach empty, he still felt like throwing up.

"Be sick and you won't get out of here alive. I hate when guests make a mess in my study, and you have pushed your luck already."

Hector's words were the most effective anti-nausea treatment imaginable, and Tony's sickness disappeared.

"The nipper had this on one of his shoulders." Hector lifted a bloody flap of skin from the briefcase and waved it under Tony's nose. It was tattooed with a phoenix. "And stop bloody worrying." There was contempt in his voice, and a dismissive tone which made Tony feel less than worthless. "You don't have to be dead in order to pay your due."

From a drawer in the desk Hector took a long needle and a roll of thick, red thread. "And once you have paid, you'll never see either of us again, unless, that is, you finally decide to speak to the police."

Tony watched as Hector began to sew the flap of skin into the book, blood still dripping from it and onto the polished wood of the desk.

"I wouldn't recommend it, by the way," Hector continued. "The knife I used to peel this exquisite firebird from the orderly was the one you handed me earlier, so I think it would be best if no mention were to be made to anyone of this evening. Otherwise that knife, with your prints, and his blood upon it, will be handed over. We, on the other hand, will be nowhere to be found, until we pay you a little visit in your jail cell."

With the page added to the book, Hector closed it and placed it back on the shelf. A single drop of blood dripped from it to the floor.

"I tell you what, Anthony. I'm a fair man. I won't even insist on the full pound, just something nice for my collection, so what will it be, Anthony? Exactly what are you prepared to offer?"

***

"Albert will instruct you on your alibi."

Tony took the bloody hand that was offered to him. It felt warm now, alive. Hector give his hand two quick shakes, released his grip, and smiled as he opened the office door.

"Remember, not a peep to anyone. You wouldn't like to watch while I carve the tramp-stamp off your wife's back, or slice the birthmark from your baby daughter's left leg."

Tony's mouth opened and closed at the threat to his family, and the intimate knowledge displayed. The words "You mad cunt, if you go near my family I'll kill you," were on the tip of his tongue, demanding to be spoken, but he quickly bit down to prevent them from escaping. Now that the business was concluded he wanted nothing more than to get away. To be at home. Home with the door locked. And the lights on. And every weapon he could think of right beside him. He doubted he would ever sleep again, or be able to look his wife in the eye. His right hand rubbed his left shoulder. He'd had the wyvern tattooed there when he was fifteen.

"But I'm sure it won't come to that. Let's leave on good terms, eh?" Hector said. "And perhaps you'll be a little more careful what you wish for in future. Now I, for one, need a shower. So goodbye, Anthony."

Albert opened the study door. Tony hesitated. He took a final look at the figure sprawled across the desk, the raw flesh of his back exposed.

***

They had forced him to wait while Albert went back to the pub to collect Gary. Gary, who had been his friend throughout school, who had been best man at his wedding, who had spent a small fortune on the tattoo on his back. Gary, who he sold out to save his own skin, who greeted him with a smile as he walked into Hector's study, and looked at him in confusion as the needle slid into his neck and his legs turned to jelly beneath him. Then they forced Tony to watch as his drugged friend was placed chest down on the desk and had his clothes cut from him. Hector gave him the chance to change his mind, the opportunity to trade the wyvern on his arm for the cross that reached across his oldest friend's shoulders and extended from the nape of his neck to the small of his back. "I'm not one to look a gift horse in the mouth, but this is too much, Anthony. You must have been exceptionally pleased with my work," the smirking Hector had said with mock sincerity.

Tony tried pleading, first with Hector, then Albert, then Hector again, bemoaning the fact that all he had wanted was justice for a defenseless old lady. His pleas fell on deaf ears. "You wanted them to suffer for their actions, and suffer they did, and now you must suffer the consequences of yours," had been Hector's reply. The skinning seemed to last an eternity, and Albert forced Tony to watch every second through eyes held upon by pudgy fingers that oozed stinging sweat.

***

"You're sure he'll live?"

"He'll live," Albert said as they walked away from the house, which was rapidly disappearing into the fog like a bad dream. Albert stopped as Tony walked on. "But I suggest you look for a new drinking partner, and watch your own back for a while."

Tony kept walking as Albert vanished into the fog, but he could still hear him as clear as if he stood beside him, "Mr. Mills may look to get his revenge, and you never know who might offer to help him."

Meetings with the Devil

by J.C. Michael

April '45, that's when I met the Devil. For the first time.

The Jerry's were beaten, and Adolf was nothing more than a rat going mad in a trap of his own devising. He'd be dead before the month was out. We'd pushed through Europe and were now deep into the Fatherland, a nation which had been promised a thousand-year Reich, but which was now on its knees. All of us expected the war to be over within the next few months, and hoped that as it faded from memory we could put the horrors behind us. We had lost friends, a great many friends, from the beaches of Normandy, through France, and here in Germany itself. Friends who had been shot, blown apart, burnt and drowned. We had seen countless others injured, many of whom would never recover, never live a full life once more. We had seen it all. I had seen it all. Or so I thought.

When you live through a war you become numb to the pain and suffering; you have no choice. Yet the experience of battle had not prepared me for what I saw that day. The day I looked Satan in the eye, and realized that evil could never be beaten.

The camp had been captured two days prior to my arrival, and the purpose of my visit was to assess some of the contents of the camp commandant's house. A message had been received at HQ that walking into the house was like visiting a museum or art gallery and, with my background as the curator of a museum, I was given orders to visit the camp, take a look, and make an informed decision as to what should be done with anything of value.

I can't deny that a part of me was excited as I headed out there. My career, cut short as it was by the war, had never gone further than a small provincial museum, and who knew what treasures I may come across. My thoughts were on art and artefacts as I collected a Land Rover from the vehicle pool, but after what I'd gone through since joining the Army I should have known better.

The camp was in a secluded area of forest. As I drove along a shady tree-lined track the road was lined with signs stating DANGER—TYPHUS. That's when the serious nature of what I was approaching occurred to me.

Not long after passing the first of those signs I had my initial contact with one of the groups of men and women who until recently had been prisoners, and were now free of internment, though not of suffering. They shambled along the road like lost souls. Dressed in nothing but rags, their heads were shaven and hung low, watching their feet shuffle forward as a way to keep moving. I slowed then stopped, watching them pass silently but for the soft padding of their steps. None of them said a word. It didn't cross my mind at the time that these were the lucky ones. Those who had not spent that much time in the camp, and who were capable of accepting the freedom they had been granted. Thousands of others were not so fortunate.

Located in a clearing, the camp was a collection of huts ringed with barbed wire and areas marked out as minefields. Guard towers, which now stood empty, rose up into a dustfilled sky laden with filth and germs in stark contrast to the clear air of the forest I had passed through on my journey to this hell on earth. When I stopped at the gates to present my papers the smell hit me, a sickly sweet smell of decay and rot. The smell of death. To be waved through that gateway was to be waved into the abyss, a scene from one of Dante's circles of hell populated not by sinners, but by those who had been sinned against, and their only hope of release being their own demise.

The sheer number of bodies, living, dead and many somewhere in-between, was overwhelming. Piles of corpses stacked outside every hut like stores of wood to be burnt over winter, and vast pits filled to overflowing with yet more bodies of men, women and children. The dead and dying were everywhere, their bodies wasted away to skeletons with parchment-like skin and little, if any, flesh between skin and bone. I was shocked to the core, and barely able to conceive that what I was seeing was real. Perhaps I had been picked off by a sniper whilst driving, or maybe driven over a mine, and I had journeyed into hell itself.

Eventually I reached the other side of the compound, and thanked God that my sanity had remained intact despite what I had seen. I parked in front of the commandant's house, near yet another pile of decomposing corpses, and climbed out as a pair of rats looked at me from within the remains. Some of the bodies were ripped open, and I couldn't help but wonder if it had been only the rats that had turned to eating the dead.

"Corporal Thatcham?" said the soldier leaning in the doorway to the house. "We've been expecting you."

Inside the house I was immediately taken aback by the contrast between it and the rest of the camp. It was clean, and although there was still the smell of putrefaction pervading the air, it failed to feel as cloying as that outside.

"Fresh as a daisy in here isn't it? The wind blows through the house and down into the camp," said the soldier as if reading my mind. "I'll leave you to it. Shout if you need anything."

With that, he headed back outside. I looked around, and marveled at the quality of the paintings which adorned the walls. They were accompanied by a variety of other decorations; a collection of antique swords, mounted heads of deer and boars, gilded mirrors and rich tapestries. The furniture was all dark wood and the cabinets were filled with porcelain and whole manner of other artefacts. I took a pad and paper out of my pack but didn't write anything down. Not yet. I wanted to know what else was in the house.

"What happened to the commandant?" I shouted back toward the entrance to the house.

The reply was a single word; "Missing."

***

Not all of the building was as grandly furnished as the entrance hall and the first few rooms of the ground floor. The master bedroom was opulent, but the other two were sparse and devoid of anything but the basics of bed, wardrobe and nightstand. The spartan kitchen offered little in way of decoration, and nothing by way of food or drink. The basement appeared unused. I spent the next few hours recording those pieces I felt may be of some value, be that monetary or academic, and by and large was left to my own devices.

Wilbur, the private who had greeted me on arrival, shared a couple of cigarettes with me over the course of the afternoon. He told me about the secondary camp a couple of miles further into the forest, and I was glad that my duties did not call upon me to visit it. The poor man visibly shook as he told me of the operating theatres, the cells and the furnaces. He told of a series of huts designed for the extermination of groups of men and women through gassing, and as the tears began to well in his eyes I asked him to tell me no more. It was as much to save me from the hearing, as him from the telling.

As I was planning to leave, something struck me about the house, causing me to return to the upstairs. At the top of the stairs I began to pace out the layout and used my pencil to sketch out the rooms. As I thought, the upstairs rooms did not account for the rectangular footprint of the ground floor, yet from the outside the building had looked perfectly solid.

Oh, how I wish with all my heart such a realization had never dawned upon me, that such an accursed thought had never crossed my mind. But the truth could not be denied; there was a missing room. A room that I found within. A room beyond a door that had been hidden behind a wardrobe in the plainest of the bedrooms, the one which had been hardly worth a second glance. A room with an unlocked door.

And a single occupant.

***

"Welcome," said the man who sat behind the large desk of dark wood. His English pronouncement was perfect, and without accent, an unsettling fact, considering his jet black uniform adorned with the unmistakable silver insignia of the Schutzstaffel.

I cursed myself for waltzing in there unarmed other than the knife sheathed by my thigh. I dropped my pencil, and placed my hand upon the knife hilt. I raised my other hand, palm flat out, as a *stay right there* gesture. I'm certain he knew what it meant, but all the same the man behind the desk raised his own palm; "Heil Hitler." "Don't move," I said.

"Why?"

"Just don't bloody move."

He paid no attention, and lit a cigarette. I took in the room as he did so. Dark, with a heavy red drape over the single window, a large picture of the Fuehrer hung on one wall, with a Nazi flag on the wall opposite. Behind the desk was a mural of a large eagle, the swastika held in its talons. The man took a long pull on his cigarette and stood, obscuring all but the eagle's wings behind him. It made it look as though they were his own.

"Do you like my camp?"

I was astounded at such a question, and could only assume him insane, although having witnessed the scenes outside there was no way he could have been anything but. I pulled my combat knife from its scabbard and pointed it directly at him.

"You're coming with me, you sick bastard. Now. Right now. Or God help me I will do the world a favor and kill you where you stand."

"You will do the world a favor by killing me? Have I not spent the last two years devoting myself to 'doing the world a favor' as you put it, and ridding the world of those who do not deserve to live?"

"Move."

I had no interest in entering into discourse with him. There was no debate to be had.

"Come now, look at things through my eyes. I have worked tirelessly for the good of the human race. Those things out there? A collection of sinners. God killers, gypsies, homosexuals, thieves, communists. Every one of them deserves to be here. Deserves to die."

He took another pull on his cigarette, and I took a deep breath to control the urge to stride across the room and stab him in the heart. "You're a monster."

"A monster, am I? That is not how I see it. I am the panacea, the cure for the sickness of man and the ills of the world. The weak need to be culled so the strong may inherit the Earth. They are here but to serve and to die." He paused, as if in reflection, and threw his cigarette on the floor. "Or perhaps I have simply enjoyed the suffering and wallowed in the pain."

I could smell burning as smoke rose from the floor behind the desk. I backed toward the door while he simply stood amongst the flames. Fire licked up his trousers. He showed no sign of pain or discomfort, but rather he smiled.

"Yes, that's it, I've enjoyed myself, and now I shall be gone. I have no desire to dance upon the end of a rope. I'll be seeing you."

A pillar of flame rushed up his body, and I saw him for what he truly was: another face behind that of the man, a scarred face with black eyes that shone in the brightness of the fire. The eagle's wings peeled from the wall and spread from his back, large skeletal wings of black feathers as deep as the night sky. I turned and ran as the inferno spread and the Devil laughed, a laugh that rang in my ears as I raced out of the house that within minutes would be ablaze from top to bottom.

That was the first time I met Satan in person, and I have seen him since, always hiding behind other faces, but visible to me. He appears so as to taunt me, yet I would not pretend to understand why I was chosen in that way.

The second time was a couple of years after the war. I was drinking a lot at the time, a direct result of my experience in the camp, and had been in the local boozer since opening time. A thickset man at the other end of the bar had been there as long as I. He must have had twice the drink as me, and I'd had far too much. As I sat and watched I caught sight of the face behind the mask. I saw the jet black eyes, and the scarred face that now bore the burn marks of our previous meeting. Drunk as I was, I followed him when he left the pub, not that he noticed. When he reached what I assumed to be his home he tried the door and found it locked. As he began to hammer on the door, I swear I could see the moonlight cast the shadow of wings upon the ground.

"Let me in, you bitch!" he shouted. "Get your arse down here and open up this door afore I kick the bastard in!"

I moved closer as curtains twitched along the street. A woman appeared in the window above the door. "Sleep it off in the shed, Jack."

He stood back. "You bitch," and kicked the door in.

He'd already broken her nose when I reached the bedroom, and within seconds I'd broken his. I broke his jaw, too. And fractured an eye socket. I can remember her crying as I beat him, his face a bloody pulp of mashed flesh and shattered bone—but the face beneath just grinned at me. Smirking and taunting. I kept pounding on him, trying to reach the features that rippled below the surface. Jack

tried to speak through broken teeth and shredded lips, but couldn't, yet I could hear the Devil; *"That's right, you show him, teach him*
a lesson, he deserves it. Just like those Jews."

It was then that I stopped. His wife, her name was Carol, buried her face into his chest and wept as I stood to leave. My knuckles had torn apart on his teeth and my back hurt. I hadn't even realized Carol had been raining down blows of her own, begging me to stop, until I saw the bruises in the mirror back home, and later listened to her testimony in court. I did six months for what I did to him, but if he didn't beat his wife again, I guess it was worth it.

***

Over the years I've seen him many times. Sometimes it has been a fleeting glimpse in the street, others it has been someone I've known. Once it was a politician on the T.V; I'm surprised that hasn't happened more often. If he'd got much closer to Number 10 I feared I'd have no option but to assassinate him. I've seen what those he has possessed are capable of doing, and there have been times I've made them pay for those actions.

Of course, I have doubts and concerns, fears that I have punished people for sins not of their own, but of his. Yet there has to be some degree of retribution, and there have been things I simply could not let go unpunished. My actions may have stopped a Shipman, or a West, or a Saville. I can't be certain, but once he's there I doubt he leaves, he's an inoperable disease, with death the only cure.

I remember the Scout master of the local troop who had an unhealthy interest in young boys. I saw the Devil wearing his skin a number of times, and ultimately I offered to help out for a while. After all, I'd learnt a lot in the army.

A few weeks later he was found dead in his car, gassed, ironically. I had told the police of my suspicions. I think they suspected me, but after finding what they did in his study I don't think they cared. I'd rid the world of sickness, of evil. I was the cure. It was a phrase I'd heard before.

Another man with similar tastes for the young died with my hands around his throat. He managed to get out a few croaked words as I throttled the Devil, and choked the life, from him; "I can see you, I can see you…"

That shook me up. Although I could see the Devil inside him, I wondered if he could see the same within me, an infernal reflection of evil doing evil unto evil.

As the decades have passed I've had a hand in exorcising the bastard from a good few hosts. But both my body and resolve have grown weaker. I've been unable to act as I once would have done, and it's hard to wage war against an indefatigable enemy.

The last person I killed was a young man who spent his days loitering outside the local school. I was into my eighties by this point, but clued up enough to know what he was up to. He used the drugs as much as he sold them, and it didn't take long to see him crossing the road one night clearly out of his head. I ran him down and killed him outright. It cost me my license, but rid the world of a dope-peddling junkie, so the price was fair.

That wasn't the last time I saw the Devil, though. I saw him yesterday. He walked through the ward I'm on, hiding behind the face of a doctor. It could be coincidence, or he could be here for me. How can I know? I'm nothing more than a confused old man who is scared to die.

I only hope that what I've done over the years has been the right thing to do, that I've been part of the cure, not part of the cancer. I hope that when I close my eyes

never to open them again I shall find myself at the pearly
gates, but I can't be sure.

Maybe the Devil will claim me as one of his own.

About the Author

J.C. Michael is an English horror author who was first published in 2013 when his novel, *Discoredia*, was released by Books of the Dead Press. Since then his work has appeared in a number of anthologies including *Savage Beasts*, from Grey Matter Press, and the Amazon bestseller *Suspended in Dusk*, another release from Books of the Dead.

You can find out more about James and his work at the following:

Facebook: www.facebook.com/james.c.michael1
Twitter   : @jcdiscoredia
Website : http://discoredia.weebly.com/

Pint Bottle Press
99¢
DOUBLE-BARREL HORROR
Just a Few
Tenants Rights
SISTERS OF SLAUGHTER

Just a Few

by Michelle Garza and Melissa Lason

"I'm telling you there's something wrong with Morton! You gotta hear me out!"

"You are a junkie, Tom! Why in the hell would we believe you? Why in the fuck would two decorated police officers believe a fucking junkie? "

"I know it's crazy, but please you gotta listen to me. That house is evil and there's a fucking monster in there eating people!"

"Enlighten us as to what you were doing in the Schmidt home to begin with."

"I was taking stuff."

"What stuff, Tom?"

"Prescription drugs."

"Really? And we are supposed to believe your crazy story?"

"It was just a *few* here and there. I made sure they wouldn't run out. I didn't take everything!"

"Junkie compassion, huh?" Ian scoffed.

"Yes, actually. I never took *all* the shit. I left some so if necessary I could go back later, if I couldn't get H. Besides, these are old people and they usually are pretty nice around that area. Morton never really gives me shit. Some of the old ladies actually feed me sometimes. We're kinda like friends." Tom gave his best explanation.

"Okay, we get it. You're a real great guy. You swipe pills from old sick people—who are nice to your junkie ass, by the way—whenever you can't score heroin. What we want to know is why you are here covered in blood, claiming my church deacon is killing people. Goddamn, how fucked up *are* you? Morton is like 90 fucking years old. Yeah, sure, he's totally eating faces. You fucking shithead. I think you need to sleep off whatever you got into."

"Roll the gates. Put this bastard in a cell, let him sleep." Joe said. "He just admitted to theft!"

"Please … you aren't listening," Tom said. "Colleen, his wife, she's there too and she's hurt!"

Officer Ian Craig had worked the area for nearly 18 years, and over time the heroin trade had consumed the small town of Glenside. He'd known Tom Fry for years, a cocky kid who'd always been in a fight during high school and became a full-blown drug addict as an adult. Ian didn't know what to think, but if Colleen was in trouble he had better go help. If he disturbed her sleep he would apologize, probably laugh about it together at church on Sunday with Morton.

Ian took his partner Joe Jimenez to the side to discuss the matter of punishment. They agreed if this junkie tried to play games with them, he would return to the jail with a broken nose.

"Ok, buddy boy. Let's roll," Joe said as he pulled Tom up by his jacket.

"Wait a minute, guys," Tom said. "I gave you the info, but I'm staying here. It's your job to deal with this!"

"No way, your junkie ass is coming with us," Ian told him. "When we wake these poor people up at midnight, you're going to apologize for any inconvenience this may have caused them."

Tom tried to squirm away but was dragged begging all the way to Ian's squad car.

"I don't want to go, man! I told you there's something in that house! Some kind of creature! It had the family dog on the ground, ripping at him, and the old lady was locked in the bathroom screaming! It was Morton, I think. He was like *changed*."

"Please describe this monster again. I believe you said it was a zombified monster, right? You are fucking *trashed* man!" Jimenez laughed loudly then made creepy noises, mocking the late-night horror movies starring lumbering brain-eaters.

"I'm telling you the old man was a monster! I've seen him before, even talked to him. This was him but … *not*. It was him but he looked *crazed*, drooling blood and growling. It was insane!"

"So, you saw this, you knew the lady was in trouble, and still left?" Ian asked.

"Yes … I'm sorry." Tom wept. "I'm a pussy to have left, but he almost got me. He slammed my head into a wall. Somehow I got away and just fucking ran. I'm so sorry. But please, I can't go back there!" The junkie writhed in the backseat unable to get out.

"Look, Tom, it appears that *you* believe what you are saying, and I'm sorry that you do," Ian said. "We are going to show you that this isn't real. Then we can all be happy, and you can consider rehab." His partner nodded.

The squad car descended a hill before turning into the picturesque Sunny Slope retirement community, consisting of several blocks of beautifully landscaped green lawns, white picket fences, bird feeders and mailboxes in the shapes of fish and family pets. It didn't look like the hell

Tom was describing, yet he protested that supposedly somewhere in this retirement heaven some kind of hellspawn was busy eating the Schmidt family … even worse, that the thing was one of them.

Ian couldn't even remotely believe the junkie in his back seat. He hated having to knock on the door and wake up these poor elderly people. He'd never be able to live with himself, however, if something bad were to have actually happened. More than likely they'd gotten their old asses beaten over some Percocet, and if that were the case … well, Tom would return to jail missing some teeth.

The two officers got out of the car. Joe paced in front of the house as Ian walked over to open Tom's door.

***

Tom was shaking, furious he couldn't get them to listen … to *believe*. Hell, he was even starting to wonder if it all really happened. In the span of a few seconds, as his door was being opened, he ran back through it all in his mind.

He often would pay this retirement community a visit when his pusher was out of heroin. As usual Tom slipped into random houses via the unlocked bathroom windows. He went right to the medicine cabinet and poured a few morphine into his hand. These old folks with their fading wits probably never realized their meds were missing, let alone that a junkie was wandering their homes. Shit, he'd even slept in spare bedrooms from time to time, eaten from their refrigerators, taken shits in their toilets. They never knew he was partially living in their houses. Tom was a parasite of sorts; he could get what he needed but never intended to hurt anyone. It was a perfect situation, or so he believed until this particular night.

While making his way back out of Morton's window Tom remembered seeing a ring two days prior on a table just outside the bathroom door. He could use an extra thirty bucks from the pawn shop, so out of desperation he was willing to take a chance. Slowly the junkie pushed open the door, checking for any indication the homeowners were still awake. These people were in their eighties and usually asleep by eight o'clock. Seeing how it was nearing ten, Tom was sure the coast was clear. Sitting on the table not five feet away was a small silver band with what appeared to be a ruby setting. *Score!* he nearly said out loud. Definitely an easy thirty dollars, which would go a long way whenever the H hit the street again. Tom put it in his pocket with a greedy grin.

Then it happened; the old lady busted through a side door from a bedroom, bleeding and screaming bloody murder. Behind her came a tangle of black lab followed by the old man. The dog yelped a pitiful wail as it slammed onto the floor. Morton, as Tom knew him, crushed the poor dog into the ceramic tile. At first he thought the dog must've gone mad, but he quickly realized it was the other way around. Morton clamped his yellow teeth down onto its furry neck, biting then ripping at its flesh before suckling blood from the open wound.

"What the fuck?!" Tom screamed.

He heard the old lady slam a door before crying for help. The once sweet old man turned his eyes on the newest prey who stood shaking in the hallway—those eyes blood-red and wild. Licking dog blood from his lips, he lunged for the trembling drug addict. Tom bashed into the nearest wall. His head spun, but with the wily strength of a street survivor, he shoved back. He knocked the creature off him and sent him crashing into the table he'd stolen the ring from. Tom ran with

Morton in pursuit, barely making it out the luckily unlocked front door before slamming it behind him. As he dashed into the night Colleen screamed from a side window.

He couldn't believe where his feet had carried him when he plowed through the police-station doors.

Now, he found himself back at the house, forced to return inside.

Tom stayed behind the officers. He wanted the men with the guns to be the first to the door. His heart pounded, but somewhere inside of him he still hoped maybe it had all been a hallucination.

Officer Ian got to the door first. Glancing back he smirked then pressed a decorative door bell. It sounded like wind chimes, and the officer cringed as he waited for the old couple in this strange situation.

For a long stretch of time no one came to the door, and Tom grew increasingly uncomfortable.

The cops agreed the Schmidt couple were probably still asleep. Ian rang again, only this time there was a faint sound inside. Tom hoped it would be someone coming to answer. As they waited, again a low shuffling could be heard. Officer Ian tested the door. Finding it unlocked, he pushed it open.

"Okay, Tom," Ian said. "I'm serious, if we find these old folks hurt, you're in for it!"

Tom felt strangely nervous as they drew their pistols and made their way into the house. Everything was dark. As they walked they stepped on broken glass.

"Something happened here, Joe. Cuff his ass until we know what!" Ian said.

Joe did as instructed while Tom squirmed. "Please don't. Please, I can't be cuffed. What if you need me? I'm telling you, there's something in here."

Joe faltered. "Ian, even if it ain't a monster. What if he's truthful about someone being here?"

Ian scratched his head and looked to his partner. He relented and agreed to have Tom wait by the door.

***

Something felt off. Ian knew Tom wouldn't be dumb enough to bring them there to try and attack them; he was too cowardly. Ian just couldn't grasp exactly what was happening yet.

They crept through the front of the house. As they entered the living room Joe motioned for Ian to look left. There, on the tile floor, was a massive puddle of blood. A mewling cry came from behind a couch. They found the family dog lying on its side very near death. Its throat bled, and ribs stuck out of its black coat. Ian grimaced. He'd expected an awkward apology, not actual carnage. What if Tom wasn't full of shit? Maybe something awful was indeed waiting somewhere in the house.

The officers continued onward, Ian hoping the old couple wouldn't be found in the same way … or even worse. He was ready to be done with this night.

"Colleen? Morton?" He called into the darkness. "You guys okay? Where are you?"

Joe shook his head; showing his hesitation to make their presence known.

"Help! Help me!" a woman's voice called "I'm here in the bathroom. Help me! "

Ian holstered his gun, ready to tend to any wounds. Joe kept his pistol ready as both officers rushed ahead. Ian pushed the door open slowly but couldn't see well enough in the dark to make out more than a form in the bathtub.

"Oh, thank heavens. Please help me up!"

The officers slipped across the floor as they entered, slammed into each other and landed on their backs. Their clothes began to soak up a warm liquid. Ian could smell it—blood. A cackling laughter came from the form, followed by a growl of sorts. Ian pulled himself up enough to flip on the light. He was nearly blinded as the room lit up.

Rising from the tub was a hideous creature. It was not Morton, nor was it Colleen, yet it appeared to be a mangled conglomeration of the two. Twisted, dripping fluids down into the tub, it laughed again then started for them.

Joe clawed for his gun but it fell and slid out of sight. Ian couldn't even get his drawn with the slick bodily fluids all over his hands.

Slowly the thing stepped towards them. It moved with a creeping, deliberate approach as though toying with its prey, laughing like it knew they had nowhere to go.

Ian grew sick and angry at the same time. This thing, this abomination, seemed to enjoy their fear. It ran a long red tongue, a very canine tongue, along its blistered lips. Ian couldn't stand to look at it yet didn't want to cower.

He refused to die like a pussy. "Fuck you, you disgusting piece of shit! I hope I gag you!"

Joe prayed to the saints. The Morton creature grabbed Jimenez by his ankles then whipped him into the ceiling with little effort.

"What, Morton, not religious anymore?!" Ian screamed, trying to make it stop the assault on Joe even for a second.

Again, the thing shook his partner like a rag doll. Ian thought Joe would be dead soon, probably torn into pieces then added to the mass of walking flesh.

"What in the name of God are you?" Ian shouted while fumbling for his sidearm.

The beast chuckled. "Fuck your god." Then it wheezed. "I walk between worlds, spreading fear and suffering. Feeding from them … claiming just a few at a time. Like your junkie, I will take what I want then will slip away into the dark. "

"The fuck you will!" came a voice from behind them.

Ian turned to find Tom holding Joe's revolver with shaking hands, aiming at the twisted creature.

It took the kid longer than Ian had hoped, but the addict came through. He must have heard the racket and crept upstairs.

The creature dropped Joe to the floor. "I can feel it in your veins, junkie … the need for a fix." The demon smirked and inched forward. "Why don't you put down that gun and go help yourself to the rest of the old man's stuff? He doesn't need them anymore. Don't pretend you wouldn't steal from

a dead man. You do it all the time to the living."

"Don't you fucking move!" Tom screamed.

"Oh, Tom. I thought we were friends?" Its voice now resembled Colleen's. "I fed you lunch a few times … gave you water when it was hot outside."

Ian grew nervous at the monster's changing strategy.

"Stay back! I'll pull the trigger!" Tom said, his voice faltering.

"Don't do that, Tom. How would I do those nice things for you again? How could I feed you again if you shot me, or let you have my aluminum cans when you need rent money…."

Now only a foot away from them, its flesh glistened as a puzzle of skinless meat and exposed organs.

Ian grabbed Joe by the collar and dragged him backward. As they passed through the door, the beast raged at them.

"I guess you have other houses to break into when you need to fucking rob defenseless old sacks of flesh! When you need to suckle off a narcotic tit!" the creature seethed. "Don't you, fuckin' leech? You're a parasite just like me. Is that why you can't pull the trigger? You recognize your own kind?"

"This is for the old folks you killed and their dog. And this is to put you in your place … I'm not *like* you!" Tom cried. "We're more alike than you believe!" it taunted.

Tom unloaded the gun into the face of the creature. The beast's head exploded then its body fell into the tub, writhing. Blood poured down the drain and a stench filled the air, like sulfur. Ian dragged Joe to the bedroom door just as the mass of flesh exploded inside the room. Gore filled every inch. Chunks of meat stuck to the ceiling, and blood soaked everything.

They fled from the house and the hell within it, then stood outside gulping breaths of fresh air when a pop from inside the house caught their attention. Flames shot out the front door like a dragon's breath. They all leapt into the street as the house burst into a raging inferno. Amidst the wavering fire came a distinct laughter, the cackling of a junkie that had gotten their fix.

Ian gave his awkward apology to the drug addict as they waited for the fire trucks to arrive. Nothing was left of Morton, Colleen or the scene of their death, though no one that witnessed it would ever admit the truth.

Tom and the police again went their separate ways. But after that disturbing glimpse into an unbelievable reality that just a few ever saw and fewer lived to tell about, one thing was crystal clear to the addict: Tom definitely wasn't getting clean anytime soon.

Tenant's Rights

by Michelle Garza and Melissa Lason

Sharon hadn't quite drifted into that deep, dead-to-theworld sleep when she smelled it again ... like something rotten and burned. It robbed her of slumber, the type of blissful rest that had eluded her for three weeks. Sharon knew that window of opportunity had once again closed, the boat to dreamland having sailed without her. Once again she would find herself standing behind the cash register barely able to function. She sat straight up in bed, pushed her blankets to the floor then pinched her nose in an attempt to expel that stench.

"Motherfucker! You have got to be kidding me!" Sharon's voice echoed off the bare walls of her new bedroom and came out nasally—comical in any other situation.

She slid her feet into her slippers and went stomping blindly down the black hallway that ended in the living room adjoined to the kitchen area of her tiny two-bedroom house. She narrowly avoided the coffee table this time, then flipped on the light above the kitchen sink and rummaged through the drawer in which she recalled leaving her only flashlight.

"Son of a bitch should've answered his phone. He could have fixed all this shit already."

Sharon often held conversations with herself. Being a newly single woman she had no one but herself to bitch to about the trials of life. She flipped her slippers off and held the small flashlight between her teeth. Her arms barely had the strength to move the old stove aside. She took the flashlight in one hand and aimed the flickering beam down into the dusty space on which the stove had sat.

"Nothing but fucking dust bunnies and crumbs."

Sharon had searched almost nightly for the source of the foul odor that assaulted her nostrils, finding that she could pinpoint its origin somewhere behind the stove that came with the already furnished home at 1121 E. Dixon Lane. Until that moment Sharon had yet to build up the nerve to move it, figuring her landlord would be kind enough to do so. But since he hadn't, it all fell on her, which only irritated her further.

Sharon had called her landlord, Neal, twelve times since she moved in. She documented each time he ignored her requests to have the "quirks" about the house resolved. She knew her rights; every tenant in every state had them. As far as Sharon was concerned, Neal was bordering on slum lord. The electricity was faulty, the lights blinked off and on as they pleased, the kitchen reeked like the burnt carcass of a dead rat—which, judging by the scratch marks on her ankle and the sounds in the attic, she was positive the place had to be overrun with the plague-carrying bastards. Now, the lack of air conditioning meant the thermostat was obviously shorting out.

Sharon half-ass replaced the stove then wiped the sweat from her face with a dish towel. Her cell phone sat charging beside the microwave, and she grinned despite her state of fury and exhaustion. There was nothing kind about it; the smile boiled up from Sharon's gut to split her face with vengeful knowing: if she couldn't sleep then neither would Neal.

Sharon carried the phone back to her bed. The odor was somewhat tolerable from that distance, and she began scripting the conversation she would have with the answering machine she had received the last eight times she dialed Neal's number.

From beneath the bedroom door the living room lights flickered on. It only fueled her irritation.

Sharon quickly found his phone number in her list of contacts then jabbed it with her fingertip, mentally envisioning gouging out one of his eyes. She knew he wouldn't pick up, the cowardly fat-ass. Earlier that day she had looked across the street to his house while checking her mail to see a part in his mini-blinds. She'd waved to his window, and they snapped shut. He was watching her. He knew he was a lazy fuckup, and she'd finally had enough of his bullshit.

"The polite shit is over, now comes the bitch!" Sharon said to herself holding the cell phone against her ear with her shoulder as she busied her hands with nervously scratching off the remainder of her fingernail polish.

It rang and rang and of course she got no answer. The sound of his unnaturally high-pitched voice greeted her with the usual *"Sorry I missed your call, if you could leave your name and ..."*

When the beep finally came, her voice was full of poison: "You better call me, buddy. I know my goddamn rights!"

Sharon hung up.

She slammed the phone down onto her bed a half dozen times, scratching at the scabs on her ankles, her stomach turning with thoughts of the vermin that left them there.

Sharon remembered waking up one night to the feeling of her sheets sliding off the side of the bed. She imagined, there in the darkness of her bedroom, some oversized rat scurrying and scratching to climb right up into bed with her. It disgusted her beyond belief, but Sharon felt totally screwed: She had no money to go anywhere else, her job was shit, and her ex-husband's credit card debt had destroyed any chance of actually buying a house. Sharon found herself trapped in an endless cycle of renting.

Her friend Marlene had told her about her rights as a tenant. Sharon was ready to exercise them but thought if she only threatened Neal, told him she could sue him, then maybe he would straighten things out and she could just stay there.

Sharon tried again. "Answer your goddamn phone!" she screeched into the phone, hung up and dialed him again. No answer. Again, no answer … just his fucking machine with the same annoying message, spoken in his girly tone of voice as if his balls were clenched in a vise-grip.

Sharon sat in the dark on the verge of tears. She ran her hands through her hair, tugging her scalp painfully as she forced her fingers to break any knots they encountered. The living room lights went out once more, and Sharon shook her head.

The air conditioning at least felt as though it decided to work because the room was cooling down. Maybe she would be able to rest if the temperature became comfortable again. Sleeping without air conditioning in Arizona is damn near impossible, a fact Sharon found out the first night in her new rental home.

She slid under her sheets then snuggled down into her pillow. The rage inside of her abated as sleep weighted her eyelids and her extremities began to feel fuzzy. She welcomed it, internally begged for it to take her to a land of dreams so she could wake up refreshed for the first time in weeks. Then, Sharon could work the early shift without wanting to jump the counter and shove cheeseburgers down the unappreciative throats of customers.

The light of her ceiling fan came on with a blinding intensity that filled her vision with bright dancing orbs. "Jesus fucking Christ!" she snarled, pulling her pillow over her face.

The room went utterly dark as she tugged the pillow away. The light had gone out again. The scratching in the attic greeted her ears again, and she could absolutely take no more. Having reached the breaking point, Sharon ran her hands under the sheets in search of her cell phone. Her finger made contact with something fleshy, and she kicked her feet wildly. She rolled then fell flat on her back on the carpeted floor.

The lights blinked off and on. Sharon pushed herself onto her ass, scooting backward until her back met the cold wall of her bedroom. She located her cell phone beside the bed. She picked it up as it began to ring and vibrate in her shaking hands. The name that illuminated the touch screen was the slum lord that duped her into renting this hellhole of a house. Sharon answered, poised to tell him where he could stick his rental agreement.

"Hello?"

"You called me a few times, I'm just getting back to you…" Neal paused.

"A few times?! Try like fifteen!" she raged.

"Yes, I do apologize, I'm willing to—"

"To *what?*" Her voice shook on the verge of completely losing her temper.

"Break your lease … There are some things wrong with that house."

"Tell me about it!" Tears clung to the corners of her eyes, but she refused to let him hear them in her voice.

"Listen, I know you are upset but you need to just listen." His high-pitched voice cracked, prompting Sharon to want to throw the cell phone against the wall. "Are you listening?" Neal asked.

"Yes, I'm fucking listening!"

"Good. I need you to grab a few things and meet me at my house."

"What the hell are you talking about? Are you some kind of pervert?" She was about to hang up when he began to plea.

"*Please* … You don't understand. You have to get out of the house. I will give you all your money back. Just leave … *tonight*."

The lights danced off and on in the living room again, then in the hallway. After that they blinked in the bathroom beside her bedroom, the one barely big enough to take a shit in without sitting in the shower. She remembered laughing internally when she'd seen how close the tub was to the toilet, but now at three thirty-nine in the morning the flashing light made the room seem an expansive wasteland, bigger than the Sonoran desert and twice as forbidding.

"The former tenants … they died in there. I know I'm supposed to disclose that, but I didn't … I was wrong," Neal admitted. "I guess I just figured that since you didn't seem the type to believe in that stuff, that maybe you would ignore it. And that it would ignore *you*. But it seems to have gotten worse."

Looking beneath her bed to the opposite side of the room, Sharon watched as something—*someone*—slid out from beneath her sheets and off the bed, landing on two nubs of legs. With the phone to her ear, she could hear Neal explain the situation. The reality of it climbed up inside of her and clenched her heart, for what her eyes beheld could not be true.

"He was a veteran. Lost both of his legs in Afghanistan. His wife left him there alone while she was out with other men. He suffered from post-traumatic stress disorder. It made him suicidal." The figure on the opposite side of the bed began waddling its way around. "He couldn't reach a gun or knife because she'd put them in the attic so he couldn't hurt himself … along with his prosthetics. One day she was baking and left the oven on. She found him later. He had crawled inside of it."

The phone went silent as Neal collected himself.

A face peaked slowly around the edge of her bed, a horribly charred visage. His left eye was burned to nothing but a black void, his right clouded and sightless. The flesh on his cheek split like an overcooked hotdog.

"We found the wife dead in the attic a few weeks after his funeral. Apparently she had fallen, broken her leg and hip in several places, gotten trapped. You can probably imagine how hot it is up there in August."

Sharon could no longer comprehend the words that came from the receiver. She froze with dread, choked by the overwhelming stench of scorched flesh and hair. Neal spoke again, "It was really terrible…"

The cell phone slid down her chest, falling to the carpeted floor. Sharon couldn't even scream as the charred hands of a dead man came creeping up her thighs. His chipped nails dug into her flesh as they had already done to her ankles many nights in a row while she had listened to what must have been his wife's fingernails clawing at the attic floor, still desperately hoping someone would come to save her from the sweltering heat.

It must have been torturously hot up there. Stifling … like an oven.

About the Author

Melissa Lason and Michelle Garza have been writing together since they were little girls. Dubbed The Sisters of Slaughter by the editors of Fireside Press, they are constantly working together on new stories in the horror and dark fantasy genres. Their work has been included in *Fresh Meat* published by Sinister Grin Press, *Wishful Thinking* by Fireside Press, *Widowmakers*, a benefit anthology of dark fiction, and the Poetry Showcase, Vol. 1 put out by the HWA. They have a novel that will be released in 2016 by Sinister Grin Press.

Visit the Sisters' Facebook page at www.facebook.com/sistersofhorror.

Pint Bottle Press
99¢
DOUBLE-BARREL HORROR
Beware The Whammy
SWALLOWED
MATTHEW WEBER

Beware the Whammy

by Matthew Weber

None of us believed in the old lady's curse until midnight. Until then, we thought she'd been off her rocker, just a crazy old bird pissed about her dead dog and shouting a lot of angry nonsense.

The three of us had been inspecting a few rundown properties in the marshy outskirts of a little backwater town called Shady Brake. I'd visited many tiny Alabama towns like it, the kind of place where nothing much happened but backroad drag races and Friday night cockfights. We worked for a real-estate development firm out of Birmingham, but all that remained of this forgotten neighborhood was a sparse collection of small, crumbling homes with only a handful of occupants among them, each strapped by poverty or stricken by worse. The boss must've gotten some wrong intel, because many of these homes clearly were built in a flood plain, and over the years the structures had buckled, bowed and molded.

We were cruising along in the company van when the mutt shot out from a snarl of bushes in a golden flash. It dashed right in front of us. I heard a bark and a thump, and

Murphy hit the brakes. The van bucked as it rambled over the dog's body.

"What was that?" asked our co-worker Hettinger from the back seat.

My stomach turned over.

Murphy's face went pale. What happened wasn't his fault, although the howling woman in rags who burst out of a nearby door seemed to think so. We pulled to the shoulder, and she rushed from a shotgun house with hands flailing and her long, white hair wispy like spider silk. We climbed out of the car as she knelt over the animal, an adult retriever mix that shivered on the ground, not quite dead.

The woman's face sagged and quivered, and she moaned, "Oh, poor Sandy! My poor precious Sandy! What have they done to you?"

Tears streaked down her hollow cheeks. Another man, unshaven and dressed like a beggar, ran over, kneeled and put an arm around her. The sight of it all tugged at me. I wanted to step forward, to offer aid, but I just stood there and watched, at a loss for how to help.

What happened next was over before I realized it. Hettinger pulled out a pistol and shot the dog.

BAM!

The sound stung me like a hornet. But the empty silence that followed went deep as a dry well. The dog went still. Murphy and I turned to each other, and I probably looked as dumbstruck as he did.

The old lady shuddered beneath the man's arm. The way she trembled in place, her entire body shaking with bitter emotion, I half expected some sort of volcanic explosion to erupt right out of her shawl. The man raised his head first, and then she finally cast a cold glare upward in our direction. The ice in her eyes gave me chill.

"How could you?" she growled. "How could you do that?" She had a thick Southern drawl with a touch of foreign accent that I couldn't quite pinpoint.

The three of us each took a step back. I'd hoped the target of that withering gaze would stick with the other two: Hettinger, the trigger-man, and Murphy, the driver. But she let me have it too, with those huge black pupils like two chunks of stove coal. As far as she was concerned, I was guilty by association.

"I'm so sorry, ma'am," Murphy said, his face slack. "The poor thing ... I tried to stop. I swear I didn't see it in time."

"And, you..." she hissed at Hettinger. He was the tallest of us, a new trainee with closely cropped red hair, a heavy brow and a severity beyond his thirty years.

"I had to do it, ma'am," he said. "The animal was suffering. It's a real shame, and I'm sorry. But I had to do what's right."

At that moment I noticed the sky darkening, clouds gathering overhead with the threat of rain. The day grew eerily grim.

The old lady's scowl only hardened. I sensed a storm stir inside her just like it gathered above, and she shot us each that vengeful glare and said a strange word: "Whammy." We looked at one another.

She said it three times, once to each of us, while staring us dead in the eye: *Whammy.*

Something about the sound of that word unsettled me deeply.

"Elnora!" gasped the man beside her. "What are you doing?!"

Elnora pushed up and rose to her feet. She stepped toward us, grumbled something, then lunged forward. She clutched Hettinger's hand. He tore it away. She grabbed my hand and Murphy's, but we retreated too. She raised her palms, gleaming red with the dog's blood. We each now had the blood on our skin.

Slowly she spun in a circle, tilting her head to the sky and whispering. The local man took a few steps back.

The woman spoke softly at first, reciting some unfamiliar chant I couldn't quite make out. Then, as her voice rose:

"May a sparrow smash your window,

May your crops know blight and drought

May the midnight clock start ticking

May a whammy seek you out!"

Thunder rumbled in the distance as she repeated the rhyme, her voice rising to a screech.

"Three nights!" she cried, shaking her fists. "Three bites!"

Rain began to fall from the clouds. The wind tousled her hair like a nest of writhing serpents.

We rushed back to the van as the lady spat at us and told us to burn in hell. Her shouting devolved into crazed ranting—words I'd never heard spoken. As we piled in, she pounded on the side of the vehicle, bashing her fists into the sidewall.

"What the heck?" Murphy said

"Just drive," Hettinger yelled.

"Drive!" Murphy hit the gas.

It wasn't until we were back at the motel a couple exits up the Interstate that we found the markings on the side of the van. The woman had drawn some strange, circular symbol, smeared in blood and streaked by rain.

We needed to settle our nerves, and decided our best move was to pound some brews at the bar across the street.

***

We sat around a table in a dimly lit honky-tonk dive that served beer, burgers and hot wings. The place smelled like cigarettes and had brick walls decorated with automobile license tags. Willie Nelson sang "Whiskey River" through the stereo. Hettinger and I were plowing through our sandwiches, but Murphy just stared at his plate and poked at his chicken. We were each three or four pints deep.

"Hell of a thing happened back there," Murphy said. We'd been avoiding the topic.

"Don't worry about it," Hettinger said with a mouthful of food. Ex-military, he sat with his back straight and shoulders square, jaws chewing mechanically. "You can't be held responsible for what happened. Stupid dog."

Murphy shook his head. He was a chubby guy with a round nose, curly hair and sad eyes that always reminded me of the puppies at the pound. "Did you have to shoot the poor thing?"

Hettinger stopped chewing and nodded emphatically. "Absolutely, I did. Better than a slow death. The only humane thing to do under the circumstances. Sometimes a man's gotta make hard decisions."

Murphy didn't respond. He just shut his eyes. I was a lot closer with ol' Murph than Hettinger, who had only been hired recently and always carried a chip on his shoulder. Murphy, on the other hand, was the kind of guy who never said a cross word, and in the two years we'd worked together I'd never seen him angry. It was weird but made him hard not to like.

"That old lady sure hit the roof," I said, wondering if they'd been as creeped out by her ranting.

"I think she tried to put a spell on us," Murphy said.

"A spell? Jeez. That's funny." Hettinger chuckled and then peered over at Murphy's plate. "You gonna eat that?" When Murphy didn't answer, Hettinger forked one of his hot wings and popped it into his mouth.

I pushed away my empty plate and leaned back in the chair. I decided to focus on my beer in hope of drinking myself to sleep.

***

A thump against the door of the motel room startled my eyes open. I stared into blackness. I hadn't been sleeping, no thanks to the diesel rumble of my snoring co-workers, but I'd been trying.

At first I dismissed the noise, probably just another drunken motel guest stumbling around outside. Then, it happened again. Like a balled fist, something gave a single heavy pounding to the door.

"You guys hear that?" I said.

No answer.

Murphy and I had drawn the short straws and had to share a bed. I looked over at Hettinger, who lay stretched out on his own. I couldn't see much beyond the green glow of a digital clock that flashed 12:01.

Hettinger snorted and rolled over. Murphy kept right on sawing logs.

Boom! There it was again—a single thud followed by a strange fluttering sound. I pictured a bird on a kamikaze mission, dive-bombing our motel room. Make that three birds. Targeting us in the middle of the night.

I rubbed my eyes and tried to compute what I was hearing, when Hettinger said, "What the hell was that?"

We waited in silence. When it didn't recur, I said, "Something was at the door."

I listened intently for any further noise outside.

The drapes parted, and Hettinger's silhouette stood at the window peering through the glass into the lighted parking lot.

"See anything?" I asked.

After a moment of further study, he said, "No. Guess it was nothing."

He reached for the drapes when—*Boom!* Something hit the door again.

Hettinger drew the black shape of a pistol from the nightstand. His profile slipped past the window and disappeared in front of the door. He swung it open and stood with the gun aimed outside.

There was no one at the door. Nor any birds.

"What's going on?" Murphy grumbled from a tangle of sheets.

From somewhere outside, far in the distance and possibly miles away, came the long, low, mournful blare of a great horn. My skin turned to gooseflesh as I listened to that noise, a deep bellowing tone from a giant trumpet like a medieval call to war. I'd never heard anything like it outside a Hollywood movie.

I clicked on the bedside lamp. Hettinger looked at me. With his brow arched and lips pinched tight, he appeared worried—totally uncharacteristic.

I shrugged in return.

"What's that sound?" Murphy muttered. He sat up next to me and rubbed his face.

Hettinger lifted his finger to his mouth.

"Shhhhhhhhhh," he said. "*Listen...*"

He turned around and gazed into the dark horizon, in the direction of that eerie wail. Mixed within that menacing tone was the whisper of a gathering breeze that strengthened and swelled. As the wind intensified, it stirred the drapes inside the room.

"What do you think that sound is?" Murphy said.

Hettinger shook his head. "I'm not sure I want to know."

A violent gust blasted into the room with a sudden sucking vibration. Hettinger flew from his feet. The door banged off the doorstop. My hair blew back, and my ears popped from the pressure.

Papers and beer cans swirled into the air. The clutter on the sink counter clattered against the mirror. Toothbrushes and razors went everywhere. Murphy gave a high shout as the bedsheets pulled from his body and twisted in mid-air. I rolled from the mattress and dropped to the floor between the beds. Our clothes, overnight bags and anything untethered were scooped up by an unseen force and slung around all over.

Then it hit Hettinger. Like an invisible comet, it struck him in the gut. He folded in half and shot out the motel door, crashing into a sidewalk guardrail just outside. I jumped to my feet to help. Without a chance to catch his breath, Hettinger was hurled back into the room, as if thrown by the seat of his pants. He flew onto me, and we tumbled to the floor.

His face, inches from mine, bunched up like a baby about to burst into tears. He gasped, "What's happening to me?!"

Something ripped him off my body and rammed him against the ceiling. I rolled again. He crashed to the carpet with a shower of drywall dust.

Murphy, cursing and gibbering, pressed his back against the bed's headboard, sliding himself up the wall.

The unseen force seized Hettinger, spun him in the air and then raked him across the motel dresser, crunching him headfirst into the TV which shattered in the corner. Hettinger thrashed and jerked for freedom, but again he rose and hovered, then screamed as he soared all the way from the back of the room into the mulled front windows, which burst with shattered glass.

I saw his gun on the floor. I grabbed it. I wanted to shoot, to help, to do *anything,* but I saw nothing to shoot at.

Hettinger flew into a corner of the ceiling as if shot by a rocket. There he wiggled and gyrated and seemed to fight a seizure. His t-shirt shredded away and flew apart. Then his skin began to ripple. His face and neck swelled and pulsed in violent undulations. His flesh would sink and rise, peak and valley, and those peaks stretched higher and longer as Hettinger's growls and grunts became screams. His skin was being pulled as if snagged by fish hooks, with many lines tugging in many different directions. Those peaks pulled to the ripping point. Swaths of skin stripped away from his body. Blood sprayed in every direction. His scalp lifted away from his head like a wig torn off by a vulture. His face became a contorting mask of agony peeled away to reveal a bare skull, red and toothy but still conscious.

Good God, he's still conscious! Still screaming!

Hettinger's eyes swam madly in their sockets as his body was skinned from head to toe.

My knees turned to water, and I found myself on the floor again.

Murphy dashed outside.

I needed that cue. I forced myself to my feet and stumbled out behind him. Hettinger was still gagging over my shoulder as I caught myself on the exterior guard rail. I stared into the night sky for answers.

Murphy puked in the dead grass just a few feet away. I staggered toward him. Other occupants of the hotel poked out of their rooms to investigate.

I put my hand on Murphy's shoulder. He coughed and he spat, and then lifted up with a pie-eyed look that showed the same kind of confused terror that gripped me inside.

We stood there a long time and said nothing as a crowd gathered. Some of the people peered into our room and retched. They called the cops.

I looked down and saw Murphy had pissed his shorts.

So had I.

***

The onslaught of questions came in waves that were reworded and repeated by the sheriff and his deputies countless times, over many long hours. After we'd failed to offer an explanation that satisfied the responding officers, Murphy and I were cuffed and driven to the local jail. They put us in separate holding cells, then interrogated us individually in a room alongside the main office.

We were each given a phone call. I'm sure Murphy called his wife.

I was by myself. My ex-wife Sharon had left me four months ago for an old boyfriend. She and I had been arguing lately over petty matters, but I never saw the affair coming. A real kick to the teeth.

So I phoned the company owner, Don Morgan, a man with a lot of money who I knew would round us up a lawyer. That's exactly what he promised by the time I hung up the phone, despite my stammering inability to explain the situation. I refused to describe to him what I'd actually seen.

Don was my boss, and I needed to retain credibility.

The sheriff's station was a small building with a twodesk office area and four 12-foot cells, divided into pairs by a short hallway. They kept Murphy on the other side of the hall.

I pointed out to the authorities many times, of course, that we hadn't committed a crime, but a deputy told me they could keep us on a 48-hour hold until they figured out if they should file charges.

I imagined all the investigators back at the crime scene were busy scratching their heads and vomiting into toilets.

What a mess. And I had no logical explanation for any of it.

"It was the spell." Those were the first words to leave Murphy's mouth after the deputies brought in three new arrestees and shuffled things around to accommodate. They locked him alone in the corner cell next to mine.

"You mean the old lady?" The thought had occurred to me, as farfetched as it seemed.

"Of course the old lady," Murphy said with a sniffle. "The spell. Damn gypsy curse!" His eyes were red and face puffy. I hated to see him so broken down.

"You don't really believe in that stuff. Do you?"

"Not 'til last night," he said.

That was a difficult point to argue.

As much as I wanted to speak the voice of reason, to tell him that magical curses didn't exist and that the police would eventually discover a reasonable explanation for what we'd witnessed, I could not force the words. The implausability of the whole ordeal scared the hell out of me, because it left the door open to believe what I did not want to believe: that black magic existed, that Hettinger had been targeted by a vengeful hex, and that if I remembered the old lady's ranting correctly then Murphy and I might be next on the chopping block.

"Three nights, three bites. Isn't that what she told us?" Murphy said.

I thought for a moment, trying to misremember, trying to reinterpret what I know I had heard. "Something along those lines."

"Those were her exact words," Murphy said. "She cursed us, and it came true. Hettinger got the first bite on the first night. Now, we're goners. We're *next*."

I scanned the place. We'd been there all day, and I noticed that at least two officers always remained on duty, with others coming and going. "We're in a police station," I told him, "surrounded by cops with guns. Seems like a pretty secure place."

Murphy blew through his teeth and shook his head. "That don't matter. You know that. You saw it. There's nothing going to stop that thing—whatever it is—from getting what it wants."

Again, it was tough to argue. I wished he'd stop doing that.

We got word that Don's lawyer had been in touch with the sheriff's office. The authorities would now have to turn us loose after 24 hours of initial detainment—or 2:35 am—if they weren't going to book us.

Maybe Murphy was right about the cops, and how they couldn't help us, but I was bone-tired and stuck in some hicktown in the middle of nowhere, and didn't know where to go in the middle of the night. I figured I might as well stay the whole night at the station. I mean, I had a mattress, and where exactly could one run to escape this ... this *thing*?

Eventually, Murphy decided he'd do the same.

For the longest time he laid in the next cell, whimpering about never again seeing his wife and kids—two little girls, six and eight years old. And he swore that after what we experienced last night it would be impossible for him to ever sleep again. But he was wrong. He eventually started snoring.

I laid on the cot and covered my ears with a lumpy jailhouse pillow, wondering who was next on the hit list—him or me? The clock on the office wall pointed its hands at 10:15. I stared at the ceiling and listened to my heart pound like a speed bag punched by a boxer. I, too, felt like I might never sleep again.

***

I opened my eyes to the thundering tone of a distant war horn. The sound seemed to come from every direction and quickly grew fierce. It penetrated the building and echoed between the walls with escalating volume.

Murphy sat up and pulled the sheet to his chin.

A young deputy lifted his head from his desk and looked around.

"That noise," I told the deputy. "That's what we heard last night. Right before what happened to Hettinger." I glanced at the clock—12:02.

Another cop rushed out of the bathroom. "What the hell's that noise?"

"Beats me," the young guy said.

"I told you, it's coming!" I shouted. "The thing that killed our co-worker last night—it's coming *here!*"

Both officers looked at me, then at each other.

"What are you talking about?" the young deputy said as he scrunched his face in doubt.

What a dunce this kid was. "The fucking *whammy!*"

The double doors to the station exploded open, and a violent wind blasted inside. Every loose item swirled into a tempest of airborne clutter—paperwork, pens, hats, jackets. The young officer leapt to his feet and was instantly knocked backward. Both cops took cover behind their desks as debris ricocheted off the walls and ceiling.

The shattering noise of that ancient trumpet grew impossibly loud and shook me to the bowels. I had nowhere to run—trapped like a mouse cornered by a cat. Pure panic came in a flood. I shook the cell door, trying to break it open. It rattled on its hinges but refused to give.

"I don't want to *die!*" Murphy shrieked. "The dog was an *accident!*"

Through all the chaos I heard a new sound, a sharp squeak that grew to a squeal. It came from the bars of Murphy's cell. The steel bars were bending, bowing apart to form a passage through the front wall. With a *CRACK!* and *SNAP!* two of the bars broke and curled into the cell. Murphy sat quaking all over, watching it happen with his mouth moving fast to form words I could not hear. He crossed his heart over and over, and I realized he was praying.

"*Murphy!*" I yelled as his body shot backward and slapped against the block wall of the cell.

He moaned as he slid up to the ceiling, then banged to the floor, then he was smeared across the wall diagonally like a rag wiping a window. With a mighty crash, he clanged against the bars that separated our cells, cutting his face on impact. He reached through the bars, grasping for me, and I lunged for his hand. He flew away again.

Hurling backward, Murphy crushed into the cement walls that formed the rear corner of the cell. Defiant of gravity, he rocketed back in my direction, raising his arms to absorb the blow. The bones crunched against the bars.

Back in motion he flew to the far wall and smacked it like a bug.

"Do something!" I screamed to anyone.

Murphy soared back my direction with his shattered arms flailing like rope ladders. Again, he smashed into the bars, pulverizing him. Back to the far wall he went with a wet slap, then he soared again into the dividing bars, and a splash of blood struck my face.

The poor guy was losing all shape, parts of him flying off, pieces landing on me and around me. Again and again, his body was pounded from one side of the cell to the other. I stood there frozen and trapped. And every time he hit those unforgiving bars between us, I could not help but think a sick thought: *strain the pasta through a colander ... strain the pasta through a colander.*

That's all I remember.

***

I woke to a slap of my face—the sheriff trying to revive me. I was still in the jail cell. Blood painted everything. He and a deputy stood me up and carried me by the shoulders while I tried to remember how my legs worked. We stepped into the night, which flashed a patriotic red, white and blue from the squad of emergency vehicles on the scene.

"Can you hear me? Are you hurt?" the sheriff said.

Paramedics and police swarmed the area.

"What did you see?" he asked.

"Nothing," I managed to say. "Just like last night. I couldn't see a thing."

The two men sat me on a curb outside and returned to the station.

I sat for the longest time as people milled around me in the night, trying to explain the unexplainable. When a news crew pulled onto the scene, I got up and flagged a deputy to collect my wallet, phone and the keys to the van. It was parked around back.

Lucky me.

***

I left the scene with the smell of blood still fresh in my nose. At a nearby Waffle House I ordered hash browns, smothered and covered, then stared at them as they turned cold. I could not seem to focus my thoughts or put a plan together. My brain had taken a beating, and exhaustion strengthened the force of gravity. After paying for the untouched plate of food, I wandered back out to the van, pulled to a corner of the lot, crawled into the back and laid down.

I woke up with a bitter taste in my mouth. Still dark outside. My phone read 9:47 pm. I'd just spent my last day on earth asleep in the back of the company van.

A stew of ugly emotions gurgled inside me. Part of it was a genuine fear for my life; another part, a deep sadness for poor ol' Murph. I also felt an antagonizing sense of helplessness—that I failed to help Hettinger, that I couldn't protect Murphy, and that I didn't know how to save myself.

"*Damn gypsy curse!*" Murphy had said.

Gypsy curse, my ass. Gypsies are always on the move. It occurred to me that the old lady who'd sicced the whammy on us lived in the little backwoods slum about fifteen miles off the Trapper Valley exit.

And the circumstances of the last two nights had changed considerably. Hettinger fell to a surprise attack, practically a bolt from the blue. Murphy was stuck in a jail cell, helpless but to wait for the axe to fall. But I was a free man, and I knew what was coming.

I also knew right where our problems originated.

***

A ruddy-looking man with tobacco in his jaw opened the door of the shabby little house. I recognized him.

"I help ya?"

"I'm looking for the old lady."

"What old lady?" He looked over my shoulder suspiciously then spat black liquid into the yard. "Ain't no old lady live here."

I studied his face but didn't see much light in his eyes. "The old lady whose dog got killed."

He shot me a look and squinted. "Oh," he said. "Elnora. Wait. No. No, you can't be here." His suspicions must have grown, the way his head began to swivel back and forth, searching outside—for what I don't know.

"You been marked," the man said. "I don't want nothing to do with you."

"I know I've been marked. That's why I'm looking for her. Go get her."

"She don't live here! She was givin' my wife a readin' that day! And she ain't gonna do nothing good for you if you find her. You done killed the bee charmer's best dog. What the hell'd you think was gonna happen?"

"Bee charmer?"

"Yeah, she's a medicine lady. She probably coulda healed the dog you hadn't shot it."

Damn Hettinger and his itchy trigger-finger...

"She cursed us," I told him. "That day out here on the road. She put a hex on us."

"Not right then, she didn't," he said. "She just marked you. She must've cursed you later. And that's even worse than being marked! It's an old practice. Old as these hills, and Elnora's got roots around here deeper than the big black oaks. You should not a crossed that ol' lady."

"I *didn't*. I was in the wrong place at the wrong time. Now two of my friends are dead. I got the feeling I'm next." The man ran his hands through his greasy black hair. "I'm sorry about that, mister, but I can't help you. My wife's real sick, and I can't invite trouble over here no ways. I can't get involved."

"Where can I find the lady?"

He took a step back and pushed the door. I slapped my hand against it. "I said *where can I find her?*"

He looked at me and saw that I was a desperate man. Maybe desperate enough to be dangerous. He told me directions.

I followed them.

***

At least Mom seemed to be doing well.

"…You know how your Aunt Betty can be," she said into the phone. "I swear, if she doesn't fill her daily quota of things to complain about, then she must not feel complete as a person. So, after a while I just tune her out. I hate to be that way, but she's just too full of negativity, and I've got enough of that in my life just trying to keep your father straightened out."

The late stages of Alzheimer's had crippled my father's mind. He no longer recognized me. His memory of me was of a 5-year-old boy, a child he asked about sometimes but would never find again.

"I know you do, Mom," I told her. "You're a saint for all you do."

"Will you be coming over to see us this weekend?"

I swallowed the lump in my throat. "I'll try. I promise." My voice cracked, and she heard it.

"Are you sure everything's okay, son? You sound a little blue. Is anything wrong?"

I bit my lip and tried to regain composure. "I'm fine. Just been a long week at work, I guess. A little tired but I'll be okay. Hopefully I'll see you soon."

"Okay. I look forward to it."

"I love you. Tell Dad I love him too." My dad's refusal to talk to me was a real punch in the gut. On my last day alive, the old man knew me as a stranger.

"I will, dear. I love you. You get some rest, okay?"

"Okay. Goodbye, Mom."

I kept my ear to the phone, but the line went dead. A million memories washed over me: a piggyback ride from Dad, a hug from Mom after my first broken heart, the walks we all took together with our old dog Rascal. I'd had a good life growing up, and if I'd had the time, I would have broken down and cried like a baby.

But the phone's screen read 11:45 pm.

May the midnight clock start ticking

I looked out the van window at the leaning two-story house on the moonlit hill where the medicine lady was said to live. A white fence with leaning pickets surrounded the place, and hanging from those pickets were strange charms and trinkets, some with metal and gems, and others made from bone. Animal skins were stretched tight and fastened to the front wall of the house beneath the rusty porch roof, and an orange glow of lamplight bled through the heavy drapes of the front window.

I shoved a hammer from the van's toolbox into the back of my jeans. Then I hopped the fence. The rickety steps of the porch creaked beneath my feet. The screen was missing from the lopsided storm door, so I reached through and knocked on the wood.

A rustling came from within and then nothing. After a moment I knocked again.

"Who is it?" asked a craggy voice from the other side of the door.

I told her my name. I tried to apologize for the accident—even offered to buy her a new dog.

"I am genuinely sorry, ma'am. But I did not kill your dog. I was not driving the vehicle, nor did I shoot the poor thing. That was my idiot co-worker. Ma'am, I am *not* responsible and I *do not deserve to die!*" I pleaded through the closed door.

She cracked it open. An ancient face carved with wrinkles peered outside. Her eyes were deep and dark as a barred owl's, and a strange herbal aroma wafted from the house.

"You didn't drive the vehicle?" she asked.

"No, ma'am. I did not." I put my hand on my heart in a pledge of honor.

She looked down the hill. "Then what the hell is *that?*"

I turned around to see the van I'd driven there—the one that killed her pet.

"Sandy was my oldest friend, and you killed her, you sonofabitch!" She slammed the door.

I did not want to fight an old lady, but I did not want to be torn to pieces by some invisible being.

"Call it off!" I screamed at the door. "Call off the curse!" "Go away!" I heard from within.

My phone read 11:56.

I saw red and turned the knob. Locked. My shoulder rammed the door, which bowed inward but held. With another blow I heard the crack of splintering wood. I took a step backward, then swept forward with the other leg. The kick struck squarely next to the latch, and the door swung open with a bang.

Lit candles cast a warm glow throughout the room. Stacks of books, plates of rolled herbs, and animals frozen in taxidermy crowded the house. The old lady was loading a rifle in the corner.

I stormed her. She screamed when I grabbed the barrel, and darted her head at me, snapping teeth like a striking snake. I clutched the gun and ripped it away.

Then, in the distance, I heard it. That damn low note of death on the march, blown from a trumpet by a warrior in hell. My skin prickled all over.

"Call it off!" I screamed at the old lady.

She shook her head.

"I said call it *off!*"

The volume of that infernal noise grew by the second. The glass in the windows began to shake. The floor vibrated beneath my feet. That *thing* was coming fast.

The old lady backed into a staircase, then turned and scampered up the steps with surprising speed. I chased up after her, tried to snatch her ragged gown and missed.

At the landing, she fled around a banister and lunged into a room. The door swung at me, but I jammed a foot at the base and wedged it open. I shoved my body against it, overpowered her and threw open the door as she careened backward.

A roaring crash sounded from downstairs. The entire house quaked and rumbled, with glassware and knickknacks shimmying on the room's dresser.

"Call it off!" I demanded.

"Never!" she snarled.

That evil bitch. I pulled out the hammer and stalked toward her. "If I've got to kill you to stop this thing, then I'll do what I have to do."

She cocked her head. Her nostrils flared. "You ain't got the guts!"

With the hammer raised, its shadow fell over Elnora's frail form; I hated to do it, but this was the only way. She backed against a second-story window, her face etched with a sneer, defiant of what I had in store for her.

But she was right. I locked up. I couldn't swing the hammer. This was not the man I wanted to be: killer of elderly women. Her skin so thin, her bones so weak. The hammer, so crushing and brutal. The most despicable sin, murder, did not seem to be in my wheelhouse.

Elnora's robe and hair swirled in a cold gust of wind. Time had run out. With explosive racket, two balusters from the stairwell flew into the room with a shower of splinters. The casing around the door tore off the walls as the thing entered with a deafening howl. The air around us whirled with flying clutter.

Terror hit me like lightning. If I was going down, so was the old lady. I grabbed the woman, pulled her close, spun her in front of me, shielding me from that damned *thing*.

And it came with a fury. I could not see it but I knew it was bearing down, licking its chops, savoring the meal. On instinct, I thrust out my arm stiffly in front of us both, knowing the thing could go right through her. My fingertips flew apart as though jammed in a fan blade. We both left our feet, everything in motion. The back of my head shattered the window. The night sky loomed down, the stars fiery bright. With no floor beneath us, we flew together, Elnora and I.

In a sudden impulse, I twisted. I shoved the screaming woman beneath me as we fell, and then *SMACK!*

***

With the rough itch of grass beneath my face, I batted my eyes open. I must've been knocked cold. The world swam around me. I remembered I should be fearing a hellish death, but ... that monstrous noise was gone. The wind had settled. I rolled off a lump beneath me and discovered a human form.

The old lady, sprawled awkwardly on the ground, did not move. My body had crushed her on impact after we'd been thrown through the upstairs window.

A crocodile bite of red-hot lava ignited my hand. I lifted my left arm to see it shorn of four fingers. The scream that tore from my lungs hurt my own ears.

I gathered myself and limped to the steps of the house. There, I ripped off my flannel and proceeded to tear it into strips and wrap my ruined hand using my teeth. No hope in reattachment, my fingers had flown off in bits and pieces, shredded by the *thing*. Yet I was a lucky man. A newly handicapped lucky man.

My hand ached and my head pounded as I staggered for the van.

A wheezing cough came from behind me. And with it, relief. I turned to see Elnora shakily push herself to a seated position.

Her death would not haunt my conscience.

I stepped toward her, meaning to help the old lady to her feet. She whispered as I approached. No, not a whisper. Elnora was hissing under her breath, and a chill crept up my spine. I drew back.

"What'd you say?" I asked her.

She wobbled into an upright position, her entire frame heaving to catch her breath.

"What did you say just now?" I repeated.

She leveled me with her icy stare. "I said you've really gone and done it now."

"What do you mean?"

"I mean you attacking me, boy ... that's really gonna cost you." She grinned through the shadows. "That's gonna be a

double whammy!" she said. *"A double whammy!"*

Those words were a chop to the throat.

She cackled madly, and the shrill sound of that wicked laugh gave rise to the faraway call of a great war trumpet, somewhere to the West—or was it East? A stiff breeze stirred around us, and all the warmth drained straight out of me.

That did it.

Every man's got his limitations.

Amongst the shards of glass and wood fragments, the hammer I'd found in the van gleamed on the ground in the pale moonlight. I bent down in the gathering wind and grabbed it. I gained an instant appreciation for its weight and hardness.

"Just what do you think you're gonna do with *that?*" croaked the old lady.

I tightened my grip on the handle. "Come here and I'll show you."

This bitch was going down.

Swallowed

by Matthew Weber

The overhead fluorescents washed the room in cold, white light. The detective took a sip of coffee and stroked his mustache. He looked across the table and asked the kid, "What exactly do you mean by that?"

"Just what I said," Graham answered, wiping mud, or maybe blood, off the sleeve of his Incredible Hulk t-shirt. It had been a messy afternoon. "The kid got eaten. Swallowed.
Right in front of my eyes."

"Eaten?" asked the detective.

"Yeah. Swallowed."

The detective fixed his eyes on Graham. The man had a stare that could drive a nail. "Eaten by what?"

Graham, twelve years old, had grown accustomed to being ignored by people of importance while drawing the attention of people he didn't like. But today was different. He had a tale to tell, a crucial message for his hometown, and he was enjoying his moment in the spotlight. He took a sip of the Sprite the officer had poured him, smacked his lips and reclined in his seat with hands folded behind his head. "It's hard to say exactly what ate him. See, it happened like this...."

***

The skull had turned out rather well, if Graham did say so himself. He spent nearly two hours painting the miniature basketball, one of the seven-inch versions the cheerleaders threw to fans as promotional items when his dad had taken him to a local college game. The ball was gold and green—the team colors—but Graham preferred the stark awesomeness of a black and white skull.

He used some dregs of latex paint he found in the garage, first coated the whole ball in primer (like Dad taught him), then brushed on a layer of flat white. Once it dried he used a permanent marker to carve out the black sockets, nasal cavity, hollowed jaw and long, jagged teeth.

The makeover was a success, although he didn't expect the bony grin to last very long. Graham knew the paint would soon crack and flake from all the bouncing and pounding across the asphalt. But it was cool for the moment, and that's what mattered most that Saturday afternoon.

He told his dad he was taking a walk around the block to show off his creation, and agreed to be back in an hour— before the new city-wide curfew. He then ventured outdoors, dribbling his prize along the way, its white paint bright beneath the overcast sky. It bounded down the road with a loud echo that punched through the stillness.

For the past two weeks, the Trapper Valley Police Department had imposed a strict curfew for all youth under 18 years of age. Kids around town had been disappearing without a trace. Three had gone missing, then another two since the curfew.

The adults in the area were stuck in Level Nine Freakout Mode, forming neighborhood-watch committees and splitting shifts to patrol the streets at night. Graham wasn't scared, though. At his age, he was too smart to be lured into a trap by a stranger and too fast to be snatched from the street. In fact, Graham welcomed an attempted abduction, because he knew he'd be able to leave that creep in the dust, high-tail it home, identify the culprit to the authorities, and then be crowned a hero for ridding the town of such a menace.

So, bring it on, he thought as he dribbled the ball around the street corner.

The Ryatt brothers, on the other hand, were a couple of world-class buttholes he would prefer to avoid. Yet, that's who came swaggering in his direction when he made the turn from Pinewood onto Willow Street. He hung his head at first sight. Things never went well when he encountered Clive and Terry. His first instinct told him to about-face and head home, but for them to see him turn tail would be like chumming the sharks. The smarter move was to hold his course and hope they were too preoccupied to bug him.

"Look at the retard," Clive Ryatt, thirteen, said to his younger brother.

"Yeah. He looks extra retarded today."

Graham kept walking, dribbling his skull, avoiding eye contact.

"Hey, dumbass," Clive said to Graham. "You're going the wrong direction. This is our street."

Clive wore a crew-cut and a flannel shirt with the sleeves cut off. Black-haired Terry, shorter and thicker than his lanky brother, had been born with a permanent scowl and always walked with his arms crossed.

"I'm talkin' to you, stupid," Clive said.

The Ryatts were approaching him like a couple of enforcers. The two looked almost cartoonish—dumb kids playing bandits in the Old West—but Graham knew they meant business and weren't afraid to draw blood.

"Where you goin'?" grumbled Terry through his scowl, as they moved together to block his path.

"He ain't goin' nowhere," Clive said, "unless he pays a toll. 'Cause this is our street."

Screw your, toll! Graham snarled in his mind. You two booger-eating rednecks can go push each other off a cliff.

In reality, Graham kept his mouth shut and his hopes up that he'd skate by without a black eye. Hugging the skull beneath his arm, he swerved past them and kept walking right on down the road. But when he heard the footsteps behind him draw near, he steeled himself.

A hand gripped Graham's shoulder and spun him around. He glared at Terry wordlessly, jerked away, turned and kept marching.

When Terry hit the ball from behind, it launched from Graham's grasp and shot down the street. Graham dashed after it. Terry Ryatt chugged right at his heels, both boys footracing for the prize. The spinning gray sphere bounced three times then slowed its roll to a flashing black-and-white as it veered to the side of the street into a concrete ditch. Graham snagged it up and made a wide arching turnabout on the Wilkersons' lawn. Terry tried to tackle him but only managed a glancing blow before losing his footing in the damp grass.

The shortest distance back home to safety was the way Graham had come. Nothing good would come from the Ryatts chasing him deeper into their neighborhood. Graham jogged homeward, but Clive stood in his way at the street corner. Terry resumed his pursuit from behind. Graham was cornered.

As he neared the gawky older brother, Graham sneered, "Just leave me alone! I'm going home! I won't use your stupid street!"

"Too late!" Terry shouted from behind. "You're paying the damn toll."

"That's right," Clive said as Graham, panting, drew up in front. "The toll is that ball. Now hand it over."

Clive had a flat nose and oily skin, and Graham noticed the kid's face crusted with more acne than anyone he'd ever seen.

If I gave you this ball, Graham replied in his mind, I'd cram it right down your ugly throat. But what he actually said was: "No. It's mine."

Graham's head snapped back when Terry shoved him from behind. He stumbled to the side of Clive but managed to keep his feet beneath him, his face off the asphalt, and his grip on the skull. He turned around to face them both. "I'm not giving you this ball."

That blow to the back had stung, and Graham fought the urge to massage his aching neck and reveal just how much. He scanned the surrounding houses, hoping for an adult onlooker who might break up the fight. But the weather was rainy, the neighbors indoors, and he saw nobody who might come to the rescue.

"You give us the ball," Clive explained, "or we take it." "See how simple that is?" Terry added.

Graham had learned from his previous confrontations with the Ryatts. He'd learned that they never grew tired of making other people miserable. He'd learned that even if he were to surrender the ball, as he'd done with both his skateboard and a hacky-sack in recent months, these two idiots would still give him a few punches and kicks just for the sport of it. But most critically, Graham had learned the corrosive nature of regret, how it could eat you from within, and how every time he'd succumbed to the Ryatts' demands, he'd been haunted not by the blows to his body but by his act of surrender—that moment of weakness—when he let the bad guys get the better of him. And then they'd beaten him up, anyway.

He looked back and forth between the two brothers, meeting their eyes with his coldest look of defiance. Graham had spotted a drain opening twelve feet behind the Ryatts. The concrete trench that lined the street emptied into an open sewer collector covered by a large concrete slab. The yawning slots beneath the slab drank up the storm runoff while the heavy lid prevented pedestrians and car tires from dropping into the street.

"I'm not giving you this ball," Graham said. "You want it? Go get it yourself."

Graham decided that if he wouldn't be leaving with the ball, then the Ryatts wouldn't either. Like a seasoned bowler, he took three measured strides right between them, cocked back his arm, and sent the seven-inch skull rolling right to the drain.

"Get him!" Clive said.

They clobbered Graham from both sides. The world spun and blurred as they pounded his head and kicked his ribs. He dropped to the street and covered his face, pebbles and grit digging into his flesh. Another sharp kick racked his back, but when he opened his eyes, the Ryatts were stepping away.

He looked up to see Terry hock a wad of snot and spit it on him. It hit Graham's bare arm just below the elbow. Disgusted, he wiped it across the road, smearing it.

Clive walked toward the sewer drain. Graham's heart sunk when he saw that his rubber skull had been just a little too large for the opening and had wedged below the lid within easy reach. Clive aimed to retrieve it.

Yet, as he got close, a low gurgle echoed from somewhere deep within the pipes below the street, rumbling beneath the slab like a monstrous belch. The Ryatts looked at each other.

"What was that?" Terry asked.

After a moment Clive shrugged and continued onward.

He stood only feet away when it sounded again—a loud but low rumbling burp, like a large, drowning beast being sucked into a pit of mud. Then came a thick splashing noise, much clearer, as though something was bubbling up from the drain.

Clive shot his brother a curious glance before kneeling next to the ball. He plucked it from beneath the slab and bent closer to the open slots, peering into the darkness that led beneath the ground.

Another wet, churning noise gurgled from below.

"Weird," he said, staring into the gloom. "I think I see something moving down there. It looks like—"

Clive dropped the ball and jerked away. His hands flew to his face, and his spine arched backward. A thick black mass had shot out of the drain and covered his nose and mouth, muffling his voice. His fingers sunk into the muck as he stared at his brother upside-down, eyes peeled with terror, grappling with the tar-like appendage.

"Holy crap!" Terry yelled, dashing for his brother, but three more serpentine tentacles snaked up from the darkness and wrapped around Clive's limbs like lashing tongues. Terry reached for him, but two of those slimy black whips groped for his arms, and he leapt backward.

The blubbery mass inside the sewer drain churned like a roiling tar pit, but Graham saw its eyes, three or four yellowed bloodshot orbs that shifted position as though unfixed in the blob-like body. Clive squirmed and writhed as more clinging black ribbons shot outward and wrapped his torso, pulling him tight against the heavy concrete lid.

"Clive!" Terry screamed, pulling at his hair, looking around for a hero. "Somebody stop it! Help! CLIVE!"

Graham rose from the street and backed away, heart galloping.

Like the ball, Clive couldn't fit beneath the slab. Not intact. The oozing, pulsing cords enveloped him and constricted, squeezing his body in a cocoon-like grip, crushing him into a digestible size. Bones popped and crunched. The kid became a mushy black mass slurping down into the drain basin like a giant pile of excrement.

And then he was gone, followed by moist, chewing noises.

A growling belch erupted from the sewer. The noise then sloshed away somewhere deep into the network of pipes beneath the town.

Graham closed his eyes. He blinked twice, hard. But he did not wake from a dream. Terry stood frozen in the middle of the road with a slack expression, his lip quivering.

After a long silence, Graham released a deep breath and dusted himself off. He collected his basketball skull, which had rolled safely to the roadside, and walked back home.

***

The detective inhaled deeply through his nose and leaned back in his chair. "Are you toying with me, kid?"

"No, sir. I swear on my mother's grave I'm telling you the truth." It was the most solemn vow Graham had to offer.

"You're saying some kind of tar monster ate your friend?"

"Clive Ryatt was no friend of mine. And, yes. Call it what you want. Crap Creature. Demon Oil Slick. Squid Beast from Hell. Whatever ... There's something in the city sewer, and I'll bet my new bike that's why so many people are

disappearing lately. Just like that dumbass Clive."

The detective's expression remained stern and unreadable.

Graham lifted an eyebrow to the officer. "You think I might get some kind of reward for providing this information?"

"Reward?" the detective said. "For your monster story?"

"Yeah. I figure it's got to be a big help to y'all."

"You expect us to believe it?"

"Just ask Terry Ryatt. He saw it all."

"We can't get the brother to speak right now. He just stares at the wall."

Graham shrugged. "I'm telling the truth. And now you know where to look. Just go catch the thing and kill it! Maybe you can set a trap. I imagine if you plant enough kids next to enough sewer drains, you're liable to get lucky."

Finally, the detective squinted and shook his head, a look of exasperation that confirmed for Graham the man was actually human. He turned back and said, "What gets me is that you claim to have seen a neighbor get eaten alive by a monster. But you don't seem the least bit shaken up. You

seem awfully cavalier about the whole thing."

Graham stewed over the man's words. He didn't know exactly what "cavalier" meant, but he supposed the detective had a point. Since the horrible incident several hours ago, he'd felt oddly numb, as if he were sleepwalking through the rest of the day, through all the police cars and the fretting adults who descended on his neighborhood as word spread that another child had vanished.

But as far as mourning the loss of Clive Ryatt, he just didn't think he had it in him. The kid got what he deserved. That's the way the ball bounces. Graham figured the world could do with a little less walking trash like murderers, rapists, child molesters, and the Ryatt brothers.

The detective lifted the electronic voice recorder that lay on the table between them. "Is there anything else you'd like to add to your statement before we send you home?"

Graham nodded. "Just one thing." He leaned into the microphone to be heard perfectly clear. "Whatever was in the sewer drain that swallowed Clive Ryatt, it's just a shame it
didn't eat his no-good brother, too."

The detective pressed stop on the recorder.

About the Author

Matthew Weber resides just north of Birmingham, Alabama, with his wife, two sons, a daughter, and a doggie. He is owner of Pint Bottle Press and author of *Bobcats, Teeth Marks, A Dark & Winding Road,* and *The Bull.* He has written and illustrated two children's books, *I Want to Be a Monster When I Grow Up* and *Attack of the Giant Mutant Worms.* Weber is editor-in-chief of *Home Improvement & Repairs* magazine and is also author of the non-fiction book, *The Quick & Easy Home DIY Manual.* Visit him online at www.pintbottlepress.com.

www.ingramcontent.com/pod-product-compliance
Lightning Source LLC
Chambersburg PA
CBHW032002180726
48283CB00008B/2530